THE PURSUED

A CONTEMPORARY REVERSE HAREM ROMANCE (SAVAGE MOUNTAIN MEN)

MIKA LANE

BE THE FIRST TO KNOW...

Want more heat, heart,
and bad boys who know what they're doing?
Join my list and I'll send the steam straight to your inbox,
starting with a deliciously naughty story:

SIGN UP TO MY MAILING LIST!
Or visit:
https://geni.us/free-book-signup

CHAPTER 1

PHEE

"**G**et out *here*? Like *right* here?"

The driver sighed. "Miss, this is as far as I take you. I got explicit instructions. It's the end of the trip for us."

He glanced at me in the back seat and returned to the windshield, hands on the steering wheel as if he were going to throw the car in drive and take off at any moment. As if there were nothing else to say about the matter.

Which, I guess, there wasn't.

I peered out the window and saw trees. Lots of trees. Trees for as far as the eye could see, with the exception of a heavy gate across the road just before us and what might pass as a dilapidated guard shack.

Why would someone in the mountains, in the middle of bumfuck nowhere, need a guard shack?

"All right. May I have your name please?" I asked him.

He rolled his eyes, got out of the car, and began unloading my luggage, setting it on the side of the road. The dirty, unpaved road.

Good grief, he really *was* going to abandon me here. I grabbed my cell and called my family's head of security, number three in my phone's speed dial list after my mom and dad.

A lump built in my throat as I realized for about the hundredth time that day there would be no more calling Mom and Dad.

Things were different now. Way different.

"Phee? Is everything okay?" Morrow asked, answering on the first ring. He'd been with my family for as long as I could remember and was a combination friend, big brother, and dad. Now, he was the only family I had.

"Morrow," I said, my voice breaking, "the limo driver is leaving me in the middle of nowhere."

Images of bears, rattlesnakes, and brown recluse spiders paraded through my mind, goading me. Laughing at me.

The trunk slammed, and the driver moved the last of my five suitcases to the edge of the road, where they sat in the dust.

My very expensive luggage. Gifts from the parents. Getting dustier by the moment.

I remained glued to the back seat, with no plans to move.

I could handle this, right? I'd been to summer camp, and that had been in the woods.

The driver silently got back in the car and pulled on his seat belt. He started the engine and looked at me in the rearview mirror with pleading eyes. I know he didn't want any trouble—he just wanted to hit the road. Without *me* in the car.

He couldn't just kick me out, could he? I mean, would he physically drag me out of the car and throw me in the dirt just like he did my luggage?

Who does that?

"Morrow, what do I do?" I asked into my cell. "I'm still in the limo. I think as long as I don't get out, he can't leave."

I gave the driver my best killer stink eye. "He put my luggage on the side of the road and is telling me I have to get out here. I don't think I should. I mean, there's nothing around here. I'm literally in the woods."

The driver looked at me in the rearview mirror. "I'm sorry, miss, just following instructions."

"*I know.* And *I'm* just trying to stay alive."

"Phee! Calm down," Morrow said. "Are you near a gate over the road and a little guardhouse?"

"Yes, that's exactly where I am. Why are there no people around? Is this the set-up you arranged? Because if it is, Morrow—"

"It is exactly where you are supposed to be. You can get out of the car and let the driver go," he said calmly.

I sniffled. "What? Are you sure?"

Anyone who looked at me could see I wasn't the outdoorsy type. I'd only agreed to go to Savage Mountain kicking and screaming. Morrow had promised it was a temporary arrangement, one to keep me safe while he investigated my parents' recent murders.

"You're fine. Someone will be by to pick you up. It's all arranged. Don't be scared—you're safe there. Keep me posted, okay?"

"Yeah," I said before swiping my phone closed. "Sorry, dude," I said to the driver, grabbing the door handle and mustering my best apologetic smile.

"Take care, miss. Best of luck."

Whatever.

I slammed the door behind me, the driver giving me a little wave before he took off, leaving my luggage and me in a cloud of limousine dust.

After several deep breaths, I reminded myself to trust Morrow. He'd always looked out for my family, and I knew he'd never fail me. If he said things were going according to plan, as he just had, then they were. He knew things. I could rely on him.

Not that I had much choice. I mean, my parents were gone. There really wasn't anyone else *to* rely on.

I'd had to pack and get out of my penthouse apartment—the one my parents had bought me—so quickly that I wasn't dressed for the mountains. Actually, I was never dressed for the mountains.

I didn't *do* mountains. Or nature, or the outdoors, or woods, or trees. And certainly not dirt roads.

Unless I was in a park somewhere, painting with my oils.

That was civilized. *This* was not.

I looked up and down the road I'd just been dumped on, wondering what was next. There was nothing, and I mean nothing, in either direction but the continuation of said road—rocky and dusty, framed on both sides by trees and bushes packed so tightly together, you couldn't see three feet in.

Well, with the exception of one small opening. And where the hell did that go?

I wobbled toward the narrow break in the woods in my high-heeled clogs. I couldn't see far because it twisted out of sight.

I needed to take control of the situation. Someone may or may not come for me as Morrow promised, but I could be a little proactive about things, too.

I might not be an 'outdoorsy girl,' but I wasn't an idiot, either. I dug into one of my duffels and ditched my impractical clogs for my Converse Chucks. Then, I walked over to the little guardhouse structure, which, by the way, had no guard. What was the point of that?

I peered through the dusty window. There hadn't been anyone in there in a long time, if ever. Damn thing was probably just for show. Some of my parents' more pretentious friends did shit like that, acting like their property needed a guard when they knew damn well they'd never hire one.

I yanked on the door handle, and darn if the thing wasn't unlocked.

Yes.

Was something finally going my way?

I dragged each piece of my luggage, one by one, and stuffed it inside a space no bigger than a bathroom stall. Out of habit, I grabbed my sketchbook and some pencils, shoved them into my cross-body bag, and pulled the door shut.

At least my crap was off the road and out of sight.

I had to admit, the scent of pine and fresh mountain something-or-other was kind of nice, in spite of my horrible circumstances. I closed my eyes and took several deep breaths just like I'd learned in yoga.

Calm.

I walked a few yards along the trail I'd spied, just past the bend, making sure I could still see the road behind me. It wouldn't do to get lost on top of everything else, so I moved slowly. The sound of crickets—or were they cicadas?—rose and fell around me like some kind of insect symphony. It was actually kind of cool. If you liked that sort of thing.

The path twisted a few more times, and the road was quickly out of sight. But if I just stuck to it, I figured I couldn't get lost.

Right?

I walked for what seemed like only five minutes before I came to a clearing with a little pond in the middle. If I weren't so freaked by my current situation, I might have been pleasantly surprised.

It was picturesque, I had to admit, and something I normally would have been thrilled to happen upon as the perfect opportunity to do some oil painting. I didn't have my oils with me just then, but I *did* have my sketchpad.

Since I was a kid, drawing had allowed me to take my anxiety down a notch. I'd get lost in the sweeping motions I'd make over the page, sometimes letting hours go by playing with my gouache colors.

Peeking into my bag, I found that, in my packing haste, I'd grabbed only a bunch of number two pencils. Nothing with color.

But that was better than nothing.

I made myself comfortable on an old log just at the edge of the pond, listening for any sound from the road indicating someone had come for me, as Morrow promised. I pulled out my pad, turned to the first empty page, and dragged my soft pencil across the cream paper.

As I worked to get the shape of the pond just right, a modicum of calm washed over me for the first time since I'd been told my parents had been killed on their private plane—a flight I was supposed to be on, with them—when I'd had to gather as many of my things as I could in fifteen minutes before Morrow had spirited me out of town, supposedly to safety.

I'd barely had five minutes to cry over them. My parents.

Gone.

But I wasn't going to cry now. I had to stay focused on next steps. And my drawing was allowing me to do just that.

It was noonish, and with the sun overhead, things were getting toasty. I kicked off my Chucks and dangled my feet in the pond below, just as I remembered I needed to call my best friend, India—if I could get a signal, considering were I was. She'd be worried sick about me—I'd only told her I was leaving town, and I had no idea for how long. She'd begged me not to, and instead, told me to come over her place.

But Morrow had insisted I go, and I knew my parents would want me to listen to him.

I reached for my bag, and my sudden movement jolted the log I was sitting on. The unsteady sucker rolled forward a couple inches, and then right into the pond, taking me and my sketchpad right in the water with it.

Thanks, universe. Just shit on me again, why don't you?

I found myself in slippery pond water up to my waist when I got my feet back under me, my hair covering my face and obstructing my vision. When I pushed it aside, I saw my sketchpad floating on the water's surface, upside down.

That's when the lump rising in my throat erupted into a full-on scream, first of frustration, and then of grief. I tucked the ruined pad under my arm and pulled myself onto the muddy bank.

I dropped to my knees, my soggy sketchpad before me, staring back as if it were asking *how could you be so careless? I thought I was important to you.*

The woods around me blurred as tears flooded my

eyes, the ones I'd been denying since I'd gotten the terrible news. I couldn't see, hear, or smell anything, the grief nearly stealing my breath as well.

Clawing at the dirt below me, then beating my fists on the ground, the anger and pain I'd kept inside for the last twenty-four hours overtook every cell in my body.

Someone had taken my parents from me.

Actually, they'd taken everything from me. And I didn't know how I'd survive.

I retched from the pain tearing at my stomach and ugly cried until my head pounded and I was gasping for breath. How do you live when everything in your life is pulled out from under your feet?

I crawled back to my shoes and bag, where my log had been before it had rolled itself and me into the water, and found my phone flashing. Thank god *that* hadn't gone in the pond.

It was a call from Morrow. But I didn't pick up. I just looked at my soaked sketchpad and my filthy capri pants and T-shirt. I didn't even scoot into the spot of sun next to me to dry off.

I just didn't care.

CHAPTER 2

JACK

"**W**hat's that noise?"

Axel and I stopped walking to try and make out the unexpected sounds coming from somewhere in the woods.

He cocked an ear as well, at what sounded like a strange combination of splashing water and crying.

"What the hell?" he said, frowning.

There was good reason for his concern. We didn't get unexpected visitors on Savage Mountain. And if we did, it was cause for alarm.

In other words, uninvited guests were pretty much guaranteed to mean trouble. Big trouble.

When I left academia and entered the dark underworld of 'private security,' as it's known, I was leaving behind life as I knew it. I was prepared. I knew what to expect.

But it was exhausting, this new life, always being on alert. The price to be paid, I supposed, for a life of action and good pay.

"What the fuck?" Alex asked, peering through the thick brush.

I looked over his shoulder. "Jesus. Who's that?"

About twenty yards away, a young woman sat on the ground next to what looked like a bag and a large notebook, crying her eyes out. She was also dripping wet.

She was a sorry sight, her long hair soaked and stuck to her back and shoulders, her T-shirt and pants clinging to her thin frame. She rocked quietly on her knees and pounded her fists on the ground in front of her.

Whoever she was, there was no doubt she was having a massive crisis.

"C'mon," Axel said, preparing to bust through the bushes. And probably scare the shit out of her.

But I grabbed his arm, restraining him with effort. "Hold on."

He looked at me in surprise. "Dude, we don't know who she is."

I shook my head thinking quickly to connect the dots. "Wait. I do. The security guy who called us last night, who works for Erickson Consulting? Maybe this is the person he said they'd be dropping off."

"Yeah, but isn't that for next week?" Axel asked.

I honestly couldn't be sure. But whoever she was, she sat, cross-legged, tapping at her phone screen.

Good luck with that. Cell service on Savage Mountain was crap.

But her call must have gone through, because she began to shout at her phone.

"India. India, can you hear me?" she cried. *"Yes, it's Phee. I'm at the hiding place Morrow sent me to. Well, I think I am, anyway. You're right—I should have just come to your place. It's awful here. They just dropped me off on the side of the road in the middle of nowhere. Someone's supposed to pick me up, but no one has come."*

She nodded as if listening.

"I don't know, India. I guess I have to stay until Morrow —India? India, are you there?"

She looked at her phone screen and dropped her head into her hand.

Call over.

Axel turned to me. *"That's* who they sent us? I thought it was going to be a boy, someone who'd just lost his parents."

I shrugged. The details we'd gotten were scant due to the secure nature of the assignment. But I'd never thought we'd be charged with watching someone like *this.* I mean, sure, she looked like a drowned rat, and the poor woman was seriously down and out. But from what I could gather, she was a raving beauty. Clearly not prepared for a visit to the woods but gorgeous, nonetheless, with long blonde hair and a lovely figure.

"Excuse me, buddy, but duty calls," I said, pushing past Axel.

Who immediately pulled me back.

Fucker. Always trying to cockblock me.

"Dude, I'm the senior on this team. I go in first," I said.

He rolled his eyes, giving me a look.

Hey, I didn't like pulling rank, but a guy had to do that every now and again, especially with a guy like Axel who had a tendency to act first and think later.

I pushed through the bushes. "Miss. Excuse me, miss?" I said, stopping several feet away.

Her head whipped in our direction, and she shrieked.

"Sorry, we didn't mean to scare you—"

But before I could finish my apology, she scooped up her stuff and stood to run. Which wouldn't have been smart, considering her sneakers were in her hands and not on her feet.

Like I said, not an outdoorsy kind of girl.

"Miss," I called, "no need to be afraid," I took a step forward and held my hands up like a peace offering. Old habits died hard.

"We're the people you're staying with here on Savage Mountain. We thought you were coming next week. We were just out patrolling the property."

Wretched creature she was, her face was pink with sunburn, streaked with black rivers of makeup. And she was terrified.

"Wh... who are you guys?" she asked, her voice trembling.

"I'm Jack. This is Axel. We were contacted by the security head of Erickson Consulting. We were told to expect someone named Philip Erickson."

Her hunched shoulders slowly returned to their normal position, and she took a breath.

"The name is Philippa, not Philip. And I go by Phee." She gave us a resigned little smile.

I looked at Axel, who shrugged.

"Sorry 'bout that. Guess something got lost in the transmission." I stepped forward and offered her a hand.

"So, you guys are the ones who are supposed to pick me up? Take me someplace safe?"

I nodded. "Yup. Welcome to Savage Mountain."

She curled her lip, like she'd tasted something bad. "Well. Here I am." She shrugged like she'd rather be anywhere else in the world.

"Sorry about scaring the crap out of you. Hey, how'd you get wet? You weren't swimming in that pond, were you?"

She looked down at her shoes and then bent to put them back on her feet.

"I did go in the water, but it was an accident. I got soaked and ruined my sketchpad." She held up a sad pile of wet paper.

"Well, we can probably dry that. But you need to stay out of that pond. It's full of snapping turtles." I watched one of the critters pop his head up to take a look at us and, just as quickly, dive back under the water.

She rolled her eyes as she tied her shoes. "Yeah, well, it's not like I went in there on purpose. But it would have been great for a turtle to snip my toe off. Really round out the great luck I've been having lately." She stood, wet pad in hand, sorry-looking but ready to go.

"Let's get to the cabin where you'll be staying. That all you have, that little bag?" I asked, pointing.

She looked down it, then back at me like I was the world's biggest fucking idiot.

"Um, no, this is not all I have. I stuffed my things in the guard shack after I got dropped off."

Guard shack?

"That little hut near the gate?" Axel asked.

She nodded. "Yup." She followed me along the trail back to where she must have hit the trail. "I couldn't just leave my stuff on the side of the road, could I?"

Smart.

And to be honest, it was a damn good thing Axel and I were patrolling the property. We wouldn't have been looking for a woman, or anyone for that matter, for another week.

Bad information on two counts. I didn't like bad info. It lead to dead people.

"Christ, all this stuff is yours?" Axel asked when Phee opened the door and revealed four or five pieces of luggage. And not the small carry-on wheelie bags. This woman had serious shit.

Really? I didn't think all four guys in our house owned this must stuff altogether.

She lifted her chin. "Yes. Yes, this is mine."

Axel and I must have been standing there with our mouths open because she continued her defense.

"I had fifteen minutes to pack after having been told my parents were killed. I had no idea where I was going or for how long. So, I threw whatever I could in every bag I had. I wasn't really thinking straight at the time." She looked at her luggage like it was going to walk out of the guard shack and follow us to the cabin by itself.

Who the hell packs like that, regardless of where they're going?

"All right. Phee, you carry this duffel, okay?" I handed it to her. "Axel and I will get the rest."

She nodded, slinging the duffel over her shoulder while Axel and I handled two giant suitcases apiece. Where did she think she was going? A five-star hotel?

Unaware that we were not hired bellmen, she supervised as if to ensure the safety of her belongings.

"How did you two come to be associated with my father's company?" she asked as we carried her crap.

"You mean Erickson Consulting?"

"Yup. My dad's company. Well, it *was* his company," she corrected, her voice cracking.

"I knew your dad from my university days. We were recruited to the CIA and started in the same freshman class."

Axel cleared his throat as a warning signal.

"Ax, I think we can talk about this now," I said.

I stole a glance at Phee, who just stared at the ground ahead. Maybe I did have to start watching my mouth with her around.

"That's cool you worked with my dad. He was in the CIA before he started his private security company?"

Shit. We'd already said too much.

"I'm sorry he's gone, Phee. He was a good man."

She just kept walking alongside me, shifting her duffel from one shoulder to the other every few minutes, a confused expression on her face.

"You look a lot younger than he," she said.

"Yeah, I am." I was eager to fill the space before she asked more questions. Guess her dad didn't tell her everything, which meant I'd better tread lightly.

"We had some missions together early in my career, before he started his company. In fact, we did some work under Erickson over the years, ourselves. And we've known Morrow a good long time."

Christ, her bags weighed a ton. She had a few things to learn about life in the mountains, no doubt about that. And the first lesson was that she needed better footwear.

"Hey, Phee, do you have any boots? Hiking boots?" Axel asked. "They might be better than your sneakers."

For the first time, her face brightened. Small victories...

"I do have hiking boots, in fact. They're still in the box in one of my bags. Brand-new," she said proudly. "I

got them for a trip to the Himalayas with my parents…
which I guess I'm no longer going on."

Axel and I looked at each other. That she had hiking
boots was good. Really good. That she'd obviously
never worn them, much less broken them in, told us
just about everything we needed to know.

"We'll have you wear them for a few hours of light
walking every day to break them in. You'll be glad you
did," I said.

Axel stopped for a moment and hoisted a suitcase
higher on his shoulder. "What's in here, anyway? Feels
like bricks."

She smiled brightly. "I have a lot of books with me. I
study languages in my free time."

Really? You're trying to escape bad guys, you have a
few minutes to pack before you're spirited away to a
secret destination, and you pack a shitload of *books*?

And who studied languages, *anyway*?

"I guess I didn't need to bring all this," she said,
gesturing toward her luggage.

Gee. Thanks.

She sure was lovely, though, and now that her
clothes were drying and not clinging to her like a mass
of rags, I could see she had a lithe figure, probably from
hours spent using an expensive gym membership.

While I'd not been in regular contact with her dad
in a while, I'd kept tabs on the man and knew the
company he'd started had become massively successful.
His only daughter was certainly not wanting for
anything.

She suddenly dropped her duffel to the ground and rolled her shoulders with a grimace.

"Here, I can get this," I said. "We're almost there."

She tried to pick her bag back up, but it was clear she was done. I hoisted it into my arms and increased my pace.

"Thank you, Jack," she said with an embarrassed smile.

"How long do you expect to be with us, Phee?" I asked.

"Just a few days, I'm told. Morrow has to get some things straightened out first before he can be sure I'm safe."

From what I knew about security measures, which was a hell of a lot, it took a lot more than a few days to untangle a murder, if that's what happened to Phee's parents.

Which meant we'd be hosting her for a while.

And that was fine with me.

CHAPTER 3

PHEE

Maybe being hidden away in the mountains was not such a bad thing.

When my new hosts, Jack and Axel, emerged from the woods like apparitions, they nearly gave me a freaking heart attack.

First, I didn't know who they were or how they found me next to that nasty pond I'd fallen into, and second, they looked like they'd walked out of a damn *GQ* magazine spread. *Mountain Men of the Year*, if they had that sort of thing.

I could see it now. Lots of denim, scuffed-up work boots, and very few shirts…

Jack, the one who seemed to be in charge, was

probably six foot one or thereabouts. His T-shirt had been cut off at the arms, showing off massive bulging biceps. I'm talking serious Rambo action, with wild tattoos down to his elbows that rippled as he moved.

His dark brown hair was neatly trimmed, and what really got me were his glittering light blue eyes.

Why did a man get peepers like that? It wasn't fair.

The other guy, Axel, was crazy tall with ear-piercing plugs, and from what I could see poking against the fabric of his T-shirt, pierced nipples as well. His dirty-blond hair was shoulder-length and rock-star messy, like it was only ever finger-combed.

His hard hazel eyes suggested there was something in his past that had killed part of his spirit.

As I got older, Dad had shared some things about his business with me, but clearly not everything. He was protective that way, probably wanting to wait until I got older.

It was hard to think about the fact that I'd never hear those stories now, at least not from Dad.

And if these guys had been in the same business as my father, they'd no doubt seen some craziness in their lifetimes.

But I didn't know about any CIA bullshit. I was sure my dad would have told me that.

Right?

Anyway, at least these guys were still alive. Unlike my dad.

After all the small talk I could muster, which wasn't

much because they were clearly the strong, silent types, I dropped in behind the two of them as we continued on the dirt road where I'd been delivered just a few hours before. I felt a little badly about all the crap I'd packed now that I could see someone actually had to schlep it. But seriously, I didn't know what I was going to need, and I had never dreamed the stupid limo driver was going to dump me like he had.

I wasn't quite ready for a nature hike. Or swim, for that matter.

Having said that, I was sure I didn't need the formal black dress and high heels I'd packed. Mom had always said to be prepared for anything, but I didn't think she'd pictured me falling into a pond and then having to walk a mile in wet clothes. Something different would have been much more practical.

But practical was not a word used to describe my mom.

Jack looked over his shoulder at me. "How're you doing back there, Phee?"

Busted.

I nodded politely but knew I'd been caught staring at his ass.

"Good. I'm good," I lied, trying not to sound out of breath. The truth was, I had a miserable blister caused by my Chucks, and the spots where my clothes were still damp were chafing my skin terribly. I had no doubt there were pools of black makeup under my eyes from both my spill in the water and my crying jag.

Not the best day. But not the worst, either.

The worst had been finding out my parents were… gone. I guess I just wasn't ready to use the word *dead* yet. Something I would not wish on anyone. But I couldn't dwell on that at the moment. I was in survival mode and needed to focus on staying safe and remaining aware of my surroundings.

That's what Morrow had told me, anyway.

Axel somehow managed to balance one of my suitcases on his right shoulder and hold another under his left arm. All the years I'd traveled with that luggage, I'd never seen anyone handle it like that.

Still, in spite of their studliness, both guys were dripping with sweat under the weight of my crap.

Maybe I could tip them later. Or bake them a pie. If I could find a pie recipe. Or a pie store.

"How many people live in your, um, cabin?"

I prayed the place had electricity and hot running water. So far, things didn't look too promising.

Axel spoke without turning around. It was just as well with all the stuff he was carrying. "Four. Four of us guys."

Okay. A man of few words. I could work with that.

"Axel, you were an associate of my father's, too?" I asked.

"No. I was with a different outfit. But I knew of him."

I slowed for a moment and bent the heel of my sneaker into my shoe to get it off the bloody mess that was my heel. I was now basically walking with a slipper on, but at least I'd relieved the worst of the pain caused by the scratchy canvas.

We rounded one last corner, and the trees opened to a clearing where several Jeeps and pickup trucks were parked. Off to the left, a kind of open shed held equipment of some sort—I supposed whatever people in the mountains needed—and to the right sat a huge greenhouse, even larger than the one my mother had lovingly cared for.

"You guys grow flowers?" I asked, incredulous.

This time, they both stopped and turned to look at me.

"No, we do not grow flowers. That's where we grow food," Jack explained.

Oops. I had a feeling that might be the first of a lot of dumbass questions I'd be asking.

"Right, of course. I guess I was thinking flowers because that's what my mom's greenhouse was for."

We rounded one more corner, and I had to say, I could honestly imagine how Dorothy from *The Wizard of Oz* felt the first time she saw the Emerald City.

"This is beautiful," I said, stopping in my tracks.

The 'cabin' I was to stay in was actually a gorgeous lodge-type building, the kind you might stay in for a visit to Aspen for Christmas break, or to Sun Valley for Spring skiing. The kind of place where celebs hung out to tell themselves they were 'roughing it' in the mountains with their thousand-dollar ski jackets and top-shelf bottle service.

It wouldn't have been my first choice for a hideout,

but it sure was better than what I'd imagined I'd have to hole up in.

I had to admit, I was blown away.

The guys stopped, too, setting my luggage on the ground, while Axel disappeared into the shed. Who knew sweat could be so damn sexy?

I felt badly. A little.

Jack put his hands on his hips and surveyed the place with proud satisfaction.

"Did you build the whole place?" I asked, gesturing across the entire property.

"No. We bought it as a group years ago. We felt we needed a retreat. It used to be a monastery, if you can believe it. We've been fixing it up bit by bit and are nearly done. Now, we pretty much live here full-time."

"Off the grid, as they say?" I asked, hoping for the opposite.

He laughed, shaking his head. "Not exactly. We have the usual amenities and a few extras, although we do lose power in bad weather. But for that, we have a generator."

Ohthankgod.

Would it have been weird to kneel down and kiss the earth?

Axel returned with a large garden cart and began heaving my luggage onto it.

"I really appreciate you guys helping me with this stuff."

Axel grunted, but Jack looked at his watch and nodded. "All in a day's work."

Cripes, I hope the other guys would be a bit more agreeable.

"Shall we?" he asked, gesturing toward the house with his head.

"Let's do it." I tossed my cross-body bag onto the cart he'd started pulling.

I followed Axel into the house and down a long hallway.

"Here you go," he said, unloading my luggage in the corner of my new digs.

I scanned my room—a simple setup with a bed in the corner, a dresser on the opposite wall, and a straight-backed chair.

"Yeah, it's not fancy," Jack said, clearly reading my mind. "In fact, this was once a maid's room. But, you have your own bathroom. Our rooms are on the other side of the house, so you have all the privacy you need."

A maid's room. I was staying in a maid's room.

But it was okay. I could deal.

"It's great," I exclaimed, telling another big lie. I turned around, taking the room in with a smile. I repeated my gratitude. "Thank you, guys. Thank you so much."

Morrow had reminded me to be nice.

"Oh, and your closet is right here," Axel said, pulling the door open to something the size of a high school hall locker.

I must have looked shocked. I didn't mean to be rude, but I thanked god I wouldn't be staying long.

Jack spoke up. "I hope it's okay. I mean, Morrow asked that we give you plenty of privacy. We have other rooms if you want to move, but we thought you might like this end of the house."

Okay. This was my chance to upgrade. But was it the right time?

"Oh, it's great. I just love it."

I needed to buy some time. Come up with a plan. Not sure I could actually live like this, not that I was going to admit it to Jack and Axel. They were far too hot to let them feel sorry for me or to think I was some sort of spoiled brat. I knew not all mountain hideaways were five-star hotels.

"Okay, then. We'll let you get settled. You'd probably like to wash the pond scum out of your hair," Jack said, picking a leaf off my head and handing me a stack of fluffy towels.

Cripes, was there anything else in my hair I didn't know about?

I hustled the guys to the door, wondering what sort of grossness I was teeming with. I locked it behind them and swallowed the growing lump in my throat.

I'd already cried enough for one day, and there was no reason to cry over a safe, clean bed in a safe, clean location. I had business to take care of. Bellyaching about my plight was not going to help anyone, least of all, myself.

As plain as my room was, the shower stream was kick-ass, and the towels were like those in a high-end hotel. So far, so good.

Aside from the drop-off-pick-up confusion and getting covered in pond scum, things were looking up.

I pulled a robe out of one of my bags and wrapped myself in it, the soft terry and familiar scent immediately soothing.

As I tried to figure out where all my things would go in the room, given my mostly nonexistent closet, I figured I'd unpack only what I needed right away. The rest I could keep in suitcases piled in the corner. But before I did, I pulled out the evening dress and the Louboutin heels I'd stupidly packed. I wouldn't be wearing anything like that for a long time, and I wanted to touch them one more time before I hid them away from prying eyes and judgmental mountain men.

Buh-bye.

I unpacked my hiking boots and the ugly thick socks the salesperson had convinced me I'd need and put them by the door for easy access.

I was bandaging my raw heel with first aid supplies from the medicine cabinet when my phone rang. As soon as I saw the caller ID, my pulse began to race.

"Sammy!" I whispered when I answered. "I told you that you weren't supposed to call me."

"If I wasn't supposed to call you, why'd you answer?" His deep voice washed over me, leaving me covered in goose bumps despite the warm robe I was wearing.

We'd only been together a few months so it was early days, but that was the effect he had on me. Although, perhaps, some of the heat also came from my two gorgeous friends of earlier.

"Good question. It was a hard day. I needed to hear a familiar voice."

"So, are you gonna tell me where you ended up?" he asked.

Morrow had instructed me to keep quiet about my location until he was sure I was out of danger.

"I… I can't tell you. Although, I'm not even sure where I am, to be honest. Somewhere in the mountains."

"Really? You? Mountains?" he laughed.

"I know. Can you believe it?"

I wanted to tell him more. Sammy seemed like a good guy and was handsome as nobody's business. And I was dying to get to the naked part of dating. I just knew we'd be compatible.

Just as I opened my mouth, footsteps in the hallway approached my room.

"Sammy, I gotta go," I whispered. "I'll call you later."

I swiped my phone closed just as someone knocked.

I opened the door, expecting to see Axel or Jack.

It wasn't either one of them.

"Hello," I managed to spit out.

The cause of my tongue-tied greeting was the man standing before me, who looked like he'd just walked off a pro football team. *That's* how massive he was. His hair was a long tangle of brown curls, and a wild beard hung far below his chin. But what grabbed me were the light brown eyes I couldn't stop staring at.

A telltale heat washed over my face, and I knew I was blushing like an idiot, when another guy joined him. Equally as beautiful, but entirely different with his older rockstar look of grey at the temples, tattoos, and large, native-looking jewelry.

"Hello," the big guy said, extending his gigantic hand. "I'm Spence."

"And I'm Reggie," said the other.

Cripes, I thought I'd witnessed perfection in Jack and Axel, but who knew there were two additional men in the cabin who were equally as beautiful?

Is *that* why Morrow sent me here?

I'd have to thank him, later.

Their grins were warm and kind, and that familiar lump in my throat threatened to return. I mean, Jack and Axel had been polite enough, but it wasn't exactly like they were the Welcome Wagon. They were just doing their job.

"Um… hi," was all I could manage. "I'm Phee." Their handshakes dwarfed mine. I mean, it was like an adult holding a kid's hand, that's how much larger theirs were.

I wiped my sweaty palm on the back of my robe.

Spence rubbed his hands together. "Did we catch you in the middle of something? We just wanted to welcome you to the house. But if you're busy, we can come back later."

I pulled the door open wide and gestured for them to come in. "No, no, I'm not busy. Please come in."

Reggie looked around. "This room was next on our list of things to renovate. Too bad you didn't wait another month."

Yeah. You don't get to choose when your parents are murdered.

I shook my head. "No, no, that's okay. I won't be here long. In fact, maybe you guys could help me with something."

Reggie grinned again and leaned forward. "At your service, ma'am."

His smile wasn't naughty, but at the same time…
Focus girl.

"You're so kind. Thank you. Hey, I was thinking this mountain retreat really isn't the place for me. I mean, it's very pretty and all… but do you think you could give me a lift back down the mountain, maybe tomorrow?"

Reggie snapped his head back and frowned. "No."

Spence shook his head in unison.

"No? What do you mean, no?" I asked, keeping my voice calm. I was sure there was a perfectly charming, out-of-the-way hotel I could hole up in until Morrow decided it was safe for me to return home. I could even deal with a three-star accommodation if necessary.

"You can't leave, Phee. I'm sorry. It's not an option," Spence said.

Reggie winced and nodded as if setting up a prequel to bad news. "You're stuck with us for a bit. But we're not so bad. Are we Spence?" He nudged his friend.

Now, it was my turn to laugh. "C'mon, guys." I reached forward and touched Reggie's forearm. His warm, muscular forearm. "You said you'd help me out."

He sat back in his chair and chuckled. "Yeah, I'll help you. I'll help you get settled in. I'll help you find your way around. I'll help you occupy your day. We all will. But we can't help you leave. No one can."

"You know, I am not a prisoner. I've done nothing wrong—"

Spence raised his hands like a *stop* sign. "Look, Phee. We just met. Far as I'm concerned, you can do what you want. You're an adult. But let me fill you in on some important facts."

God, I wish he'd quit looking at me with those eyes…

"We guys here—Jack, Axel, Reggie, and me—are not bodyguards. We're way more. And when we're tasked with protecting someone, as we have been with you, you'll find yourself giving up certain freedoms. A bodyguard goes where their principal is. Not us. In our system, we control the scenarios to make sure our clients stay alive. Do you understand?"

I nodded, my eyes narrowing. "And if I say fuck it and walk out the door?"

Spence took a deep breath and spread his hands out on his massive thighs, his body obviously saying it was my call in the end.

Reggie joined in. "It looks like you have not been fully briefed on the situation you're currently in. But let me ask you this. Do you know what your father did for a living?"

He leaned closer and damn him, he smelled so good. They both did. Nothing fancy, just plain old soap and clean guys.

"I know a little about my father's business dealings. Mostly, you know, providing security services around the world. I guess there was a dark side to it, but not really anything beyond that," I replied. "Regardless, I still think I'd be better off in a hotel with restaurants and shops nearby. It's not necessary to be in a place this remote. It's just a little… overkill."

I appreciated how everyone wanted me safe. I really did. But c'mon, hiding on a mountain? That was Unabomber-level shit.

"Okay. Let me spell some things out for you. First, you were supposed to be on that plane with your parents, right?" Reggie asked.

I nodded slowly. Where was he going with this?

"Yes. I'm lucky to be here right now—I know that. But Dad is gone, and so is Mom. Whoever did it accomplished their goal."

Spence held up one finger. "That's where you are *wrong*."

I must have looked skeptical.

"Whoever did it wanted to bury your dad's business," he said.

I nodded. "Okay. But I still don't get how it involves me."

"Aren't you set to inherit the business from your dad?"

I shrugged. "I guess. I've not discussed any will stuff with the lawyers yet."

"Bingo," Reggie said, crossing his arms tightly. "But with you still alive, the business lives on. What I'm saying, Phee, is that whoever killed your parents needs to get rid of you, too."

His lips pressed into a tight line.

I looked back and forth at both guys as their words sunk in, washing over me and taking me to a place I didn't belong. This was not happening. It *couldn't* be.

The room started to move, and the acid churning in my stomach began to rise up my throat.

"Excuse me," I mumbled, running to the bathroom where I got violently sick.

They waited outside the door while I composed myself.

"Sorry to push you over the edge, Phee, but these people want you out of the way. You need to know that and understand that you are not safe. You need to get on board with your thinking. This is not the time to question the people who are looking out for you, no matter how much you may be used to doing just that," Spence added.

Well, shit. The men had just hit me with a slow-motion sledgehammer. And when it collided with my sensibilities, I retched all over again.

How could I have been so stupid to not see the reality of the position my father's death had left me in?

I got it now. The guys had spelled things out in a way that the more diplomatic—and protective—Morrow never would have.

And there was one thing I was sure of.

If I were indeed in such dire peril, I wasn't going to sit around and let other people make decisions for me.

CHAPTER 4

AXEL

"Yo," I said to the other guys when I reached the breakfast table. "Where's our new guest?"

Spence shook his head. "Dunno, Axe. I think at last night's dinner we told her breakfast was at eight, didn't we?"

Jack passed me the huge tray of eggs and bacon, and I loaded up.

"Funny she's not here. Didn't she say she was a morning person?"

Reggie entered with a fresh pot of coffee. "Think we should go check on her?"

I shook my head. "She's probably just sleeping in. She's been through a lot."

But as I thought about Phee while I ate, I found I was curious about her absence. I poured a cup of coffee to use as an excuse to knock on her door.

I stood from the table. "Be right back, guys. We'll have the answer to our question momentarily."

I crossed the courtyard the house had been built around, the quickest shortcut to Phee's room. When I reached her door, I pressed my ear up against it.

Wow, she was a quiet sleeper. I knocked.

"Phee? I brought you some coffee. It's Axel."

Still nothing. I waited and then knocked again.

"Phee? Hello?"

I turned the knob and slowly pushed open her door.

With the shutters closed, the room was nearly pitch-black. I flipped on the light, hoping I wouldn't startle her.

But there was no one to startle.

She wasn't there.

Her bed was made up. Actually, it looked like it hadn't ever been slept in. All her luggage seemed to be there, with the exception of the large duffel she'd tried to carry herself the day before.

"Phee? I called, running into the room and then the bathroom.

Fuck.

"Bad news, guys," I announced, racing back to the dining room.

Everyone looked up.

Realization crossed Jack's face and he slammed his

hand on the table. "Oh, for Christ's sake. Are you *serious*, Axel? Not even here twenty-four hours and she's gone. Goddammit. Morrow's gonna have our heads."

He retraced my steps to her room, as if he might find her where I hadn't.

"Where could she have gone?" Spence asked, pulling on his beard.

Just then Jack returned, waving a piece of paper in his hand.

"Now that I think of it, Reg and I should have foreseen this. She asked me yesterday if we'd help her get out of here. I thought we'd convinced her of how much danger she was in, and that she wouldn't have dared leave," Spence said.

Jack was studying the piece of paper in his hand. "She left a note. She thanks us for our help and promises to come back for the rest of her luggage as soon as possible."

"Fuck me," Reggie said.

"Oh," Jack added, referring to Phee's note, "she apologizes for borrowing one of our cars and promises to make it up to us. Apparently, she went off to meet some boyfriend."

Boyfriend? What boyfriend?

"That's messed up. If she had someone like that, why would he let her leave a safe haven?" I asked.

"Who knows, Axe. He could be a dick. Or stupid. Or both," Jack said, shrugging. "Her father apparently didn't share with her as much of the bad side of the business as he might have."

"Hey, guys? I just so happen to have her cell number," Reggie said. "And another thing. I *might* have put a tracking app on her phone just in case something like this happened."

I turned to him. "You *might* have? Or you *did*?"

He nodded sheepishly. "I *did*."

"How the hell did you do that? And when?" I asked him.

"When she helped clean up after dinner last night, I sneaked over to her room and took care of business. You can thank me now," he said, taking a deep bow.

"Glad someone's thinking with something other than their little head," Jack said.

Spence threw his hands up. "Fuck you, dude. Like you didn't notice how freaking gorgeous she was."

"All right," I said, holding my hands up. "Let's call her, and while we do, Reggie, find out where the hell she's taken off to with the tracker. Let's nip this little situation in the bud before it gets any worse than it already is."

And before Morrow found out.

I barreled down the mountain in one of our Jeeps, doubly pissed that the car Phee had helped herself to happened to have been *mine*.

Of course.

"Call her again, man," I said to Spence.

"Axe, I just did," he replied, shaking his head. "She's not gonna answer a call from us. Every one I've made has gone straight to voicemail."

"What a little shit," I said. "Here we are, trying to help the woman, and she does *this*? Does she have *no* idea of the danger she's in?"

Spence patted my shoulder. "Take it easy, dude. She's naïve, is all. She's not out to fuck with anyone. I don't think she has it in her."

Spence's phone rang, and he put it on speaker.

It was Reggie, his voice cutting in and out, staticky from the surrounding mountains. "Okay, I can't be one hundred percent certain yet, but she seems to be heading for the airfield just outside of town."

Holy shit. Where the hell did she think she was going? It was a private airfield. You couldn't just walk in there and buy a ticket.

Spence was right. I felt for her. I really did. Poor girl lost her parents and then got scooped out of her home and dumped with us, where she was so clearly out of her element. I'd probably exercise bad judgment, too, if I were in her situation.

But that didn't make things any better. We had to find her. Like they used to say in my training days, *failure was not an option.*

"Call her again, Spence," I said, driving faster.

"Roger that, buddy," he acknowledged, redialing over and over.

Finally, on our ninth or tenth attempt, Phee's crackly voice came on.

"You guys need to stop calling me. I am *fine!*" she cried.

"Phee, where are you? Please tell us."

"Is that you, Spence? Hey! I'm meeting a friend who's taking me to a safe place. Much safer than yours. So, don't worry. I'll be fine."

"Phee, we know you're headed for an airfield. Please don't go anywhere."

"What? How do you know that? Did you follow me? You guys are stalkers, that's what you are." She clicked her tongue.

The buzz of small planes was getting louder in the background, signaling her arrival.

"Phee, it's me, Axel," I said. "Don't get on a plane. I'm serious. You're going to end up just like your parents. I'm not saying that to scare you. It's the honest truth."

"I appreciate that, Axel. But I'm going somewhere safe. Very safe. With my boyfriend, Sammy. Well, he's sort of my boyfriend. But he's smart and knows a lot of people. He can take care of things."

I needed to stall for time. A classic tactic, that's the first thing they taught in crisis negotiation.

"Phee, he's a lucky guy, this Sammy. Tell me, how long have you been going out?" I asked.

I glanced at Spence, who nodded.

"Oh, not that long," she said breezily. "Only a couple months, really."

"Damn. This guy moves fast. He must be pretty awesome."

We were ten minutes from the airfield. If I could keep her on the phone, we'd have a chance at catching up.

"What's Sammy's last name?"

"God, you guys are nosy," she laughed. "Reddington. Now do you need anything else, or can I go?"

Spence began to type furiously into his phone. "That's a fake-ass sounding name, if you ask me," he whispered. "Fuck, look at this," he said, holding up a picture from Interpol of a man with several aliases, one of which happened to be Sammy Reddington.

"Jesus," I mumbled and pressed harder on the gas.

"Phee, I have to tell you something very important, okay?" Spence said. "Will you listen carefully?"

"Yeah, go ahead. I have to hang up soon, though. I've reached... my destination." She giggled. "Oh, there's Sammy!"

"Phee, listen to me. I'm forwarding you a photo from Interpol. Your guy Sammy is a known assassin—"

"Oh, god, Spence, don't be ridiculous. Seriously. And people say I'm a drama queen," she said. "I mean, Sammy works in... finance or something like that. Investments, maybe?"

"Phee, I just sent you the picture. Is this the guy you are saying is your boyfriend?"

"Oh, for heaven's sake. Hold on, it's coming through right now—"

A gasp came from the other end of the line. "Wait a minute. This must be a mistake…"

"It's not, Phee," I said as calmly as possible.

"Oh, god. Oh god. It's him. You guys are right. It's him," she said, her voice cracking. "Wh… what do I do? What do I do now? I'm such a fucking idiot."

"Phee, do not get on that plane. Please. Just do not get on that plane."

CHAPTER 5

PHEE

"**P**lay it cool, Phee," Spence said.

Play it cool? Was he kidding? The guy I thought was my boyfriend turns out to be an assassin, and I was supposed to act like business as usual? I'd be lucky if I didn't pass out from a panic attack.

He'd been to my apartment. Been curious about Dad's business.

Very curious. And when I suggested he meet my parents, he always had a reason why not. In fact, since the relationship was so young, he suggested neither of us tell our families. Friends were okay. Just not families.

How stupid was I?

Had he played a role in my mom and dad's deaths?

The person I'd been seeing, and jonesing to have sex with, was actually out to kill me. In what world does that happen, outside of something like *Mission Impossible* or *The Bourne Identity*?

When did my life become a clichéd thriller movie?

I swiped my phone closed and plastered a smile on my face as Sammy approached the Jeep I'd 'borrowed' from the guys.

As he grew closer, I searched his face for signs of evil.

But there were none. He was just flat-out handsome. Was my 'bad guy' detector that off, or was he just that good a manipulator?

"Babe!" he said, leaning into the driver-side window to give me a kiss. "Let's get the hell out of here."

I forced a smile and grabbed the door handle. "Um, hi, baby," I forced myself to say. I swallowed hard to ward off my growing nausea.

"What's wrong, Phee? You look kind of woozy," he said.

Think quick.

Nodding, I pulled my hand to my forehead. "I am feeling kind of crummy. I think it might have been what those mountain guys fed me. Bad deer meat or something."

He pushed my hand out of the way and felt my forehead. "Oh, yeah. You're totally clammy. C'mon. We'll get you some nice cool water on the plane. The pilot's waiting for us. See?" he asked, pointing.

The pilot *was* waiting. In fact, he was watching our every move.

My fingers tightened on the steering wheel until my knuckles turned white. I hoped Sammy wouldn't notice, but at that point, I had little control over my body.

Panic was in charge. And it wasn't going well.

My head spun with possibilities. I could get on that plane and end up dead.

Scratch that.

I could run from Sammy and end up dead.

Scratch that.

I could just roll up the car windows and wait for Spence and Axel to arrive.

I'd still probably end up dead.

But I could stall…

I pushed the car door open, and, with my first step on the tarmac, I fake-stumbled to my knees.

"Oh, damn, ouch, look what I did." I pushed myself up and clasped my stomach for emphasis.

Sammy crouched at my side. "Jesus. Let's help you up."

I clasped my hand over my mouth and fake-retched.

"Ohhhh," I groaned. "I guess I really am ill."

Sammy put an arm around me and tried to help me back up. But I kept my weight in my knees.

"Ohhh, okay, let's try this again," I said weakly.

This time, he had a better grip on me. Actually, he had a really tight grip on me. "Let's get you on the plane. You'll feel better," he said, starting to walk.

So, I stumbled again. "Wait. I just want to go to the ladies' room over in the hangar."

He pulled me toward the plane. "Just go on the on board," he said impatiently.

I saw the pilot look at his watch.

I eased out of Sammy's arms. "No. I'll go here. Just hang on." I walked slowly toward the restrooms with my bag in a death grip under my arm, my cell phone ringing nonstop.

"Who the fuck is calling you?" Sammy asked, close on my heels. "And hurry up. We've got to go."

The door to the ladies' room was on the exterior, like the ones they had at gas stations. Not that I ever went to the bathroom in gas stations.

Before I pulled it closed, I called over my shoulder to him, "It's probably just India. I can call her later."

Confusion crossed his face as the door closed. I'd half expected him to come in with me, but when he didn't, I turned the dead bolt on the door very slowly and carefully. Thankfully, it didn't make a sound.

I was alone. Now what?

Fuck, fuck, fuck.

I tore through my bag and saw the calls had all come from Spence. Where the hell was he?

I could see from the shadow under the door that Sammy was just outside. I couldn't risk him hearing me on the phone, so I tapped out a message to Spence.

hiding in the ladies room please hurry

3 mins away. where is sammy?

outside bathroom, waiting

Sammy pounded hard on the bathroom door. "Phee! What are you doing in there? We need to *go*!" he yelled. "The pilot's getting pissed."

I knew it would be only seconds until he started pulling on the door to find it locked.

I put on my best fake-sick voice. "Hang on, honey. I'm going to the bathroom. I feel better already."

I'd met Sammy not long before, through my friend, India. Apparently, they'd gone to college together or something like that.

Cripes, was her life in danger, too? She certainly had no idea who he really was. Wait until she found out he was a freaking assassin, wanted by Interpol.

How did my life get so messed up in such a short period of time? The mountain guys were going to kill me for leaving. If Sammy didn't kill me first.

I'd only wanted to be with someone I felt safe with. The guys weren't horrible—just a bit on the stern side, bordering on mean, actually.

"Babe? What the hell?"

Time was up. Sammy yanked on the bathroom door, and when he found it locked, lost his shit and started pounding.

"Open the goddamn door, Phee!"

All signs of the sweet, easy-going guy I'd been dating were quickly disappearing.

I looked around the bathroom in a panic. There was nowhere to go. I was essentially in a cinder block cell with a very strong door keeping out someone who not only wanted to kill me but had probably also had a hand in killing my father and mother. I huddled in the corner, making myself as small as possible.

As if that were going to do a damn thing.

"Sammy, I told you I'm going to the bathroom. I'm on the actual toilet," I lied.

He yanked on the door handle so hard, the cinder blocks vibrated. What if he shot the lock, like they did in the movies? He'd be in the bathroom in seconds, and it would be *time's up* for me.

My phone vibrated.

we're pulling in. get as far away from the bathroom door as possible. gunfire will be exchanged

I pressed myself harder into the corner, like it would do any good, when I heard shouting.

"Step away from the door! Put your hands on your head and get on your knees!" It was Axel's voice.

Ohmygod.

"Fuck you, man," Sammy yelled.

Shots rang, including one I heard ricochet off the steel bathroom door. I buried my face in my hands, praying whatever the hell was going on would end soon, preferably with me alive.

More shots fired, and someone screamed.

Oh god. Who was shot?

I didn't know whether to hope it had been Sammy or not. Could I really wish that on someone, even if he were trying to kill me?

Spence was just outside the bathroom. "Phee, you can come out now," he said in a calm voice. "The scene is secure."

But I couldn't move. How did I know I could trust *him*? Everything in my life had been turned upside down.

"I... I... " I could hardly breathe. I sank to my butt and took several deep breaths.

A text vibrated my phone, which I picked up with shaking hands.

you're safe now. sammy and the pilot are down

Oh god, oh god, I chanted to myself as I pushed myself up on rubbery legs. I eased toward the door, and when I was right next to it, I froze. I wasn't ready to open it wide to see what was on the other side.

"Hello?" I croaked in a small voice.

"Phee, you're safe now," Spence said gently. "I promise."

I turned the dead bolt on the bathroom door. As soon as I'd flipped it, the door swung open, letting in a flood of daylight.

Spence eased in, his massive physique nearly blocking the sun, his weapon drawn. That was the last thing I remembered before waking up in the back of the Jeep.

"Phee, here, try a sip of water." Spence hovered next to me.

I tried to sit up but fell right back onto the seat.

"Shit. Oh, my god. What happened?"

I let him pour a couple drops of water into my mouth and swallowed, trying to chase the cobwebs from my brain.

He placed a hand on my shoulder, slowly helping

me sit up. "You passed out. Can't blame you. You've been through a lot and were in shock."

I rubbed my eyes and looked out the car window, then quickly squeezed them shut.

There was a body. And a lot of blood, gleaming like oil on the asphalt.

"Oh, my god," I said, my shoulders shaking uncontrollably. "Is he… is he…?" Then, the sobs came.

I buried my face in my hands and wailed, the losses of the last few days hitting me with a fury I didn't know how I'd survive.

That the guy I'd been dating turned out to be someone intent on taking me down was bad enough.

But my parents being gone? There were no words to describe it.

Grief steamrolled me while I rocked back and forth as if that would offload some of the pain. I lost track of time and didn't even know if Spence were still there. It didn't matter. I was alone in the world. I had nothing and no one.

Everything I'd inherit from my parents' estate? I didn't want it. It was worth nothing without them. It hadn't bought them longer lives. It hadn't bought them more time with me, their only daughter.

So, how much fucking good was any of it?

CHAPTER 6

SPENCE

Once we'd arrived back on the mountain, I helped Phee out of the car and up to the cabin. She was ashen and shaking, and on the trip back, we'd had to stop twice and pull over for her to get sick.

As infuriating as her running off had been, I felt for her. The grief was hitting her, and it wasn't being kind. Not that grief was ever kind. I knew that firsthand.

Sympathy aside, I hoped she'd learned her lesson.

"Phee, let me help," I said, putting one arm around her shoulders and holding her hand with the other as I guided her to the house.

She was small and vulnerable in my arms. My years in special ops, and then private security, had exposed me to many people crippled by loss. Some got over it. Some never did.

Life was unkind that way. I'd seen men far stronger than me brought down to drunken wrecks by grief. And as if the initial loss wasn't enough, the loss of self that followed could be even crueler.

That might be how things would go for Phee. Or she could survive. Thrive, even. Only time would tell. But I know I'd do what I could to help her get her strength back. She was a nice girl and deserved a chance. That is, as long as she played by our rules. Which wasn't too much to ask.

"Thank you, Spence," she said in a choked whisper.

We walked to her room. "Dinner will be in an hour or so. Why don't you get cleaned up and rest?"

She nodded, and without a word, entered her room and closed the door.

I returned to the kitchen, where Reggie was making dinner.

"Yo, Spence. Guess you had quite the day, huh?" he asked, stirring something in a huge pot on the stove. "Axe said things got hairy?"

"Holy shit. Understatement. I haven't had a shoot-out like that in… I don't know how long. When the pilot suddenly pulled a goddamn Uzi out of the plane… let's just say we're lucky Axel's good with his Glock. Who knew when we woke up this morning, we'd be facing such a shit show?" I poured myself a big glass of red wine. "Hey, where is my wingman, anyway?"

Reggie gestured outside. "I think he's hitting the weights. You know how he likes to work the pressure off."

"How's Phee?" Jack asked, joining me at the table and grabbing himself a glass.

I sucked in a deep breath. "It was rough on her—I'm not gonna lie. I think when the reality of the situation finally dawned on her, it turned out to be a trauma of epic proportion. I mean, losing your parents like that? How fucked. And then, to find the guy you thought liked you was working for the other side?"

Jack shook his head. "Well, I suppose she'll think hard before she 'borrows' one of our cars and takes off again."

"Christ, I hope so. I mean, it's clear she's not thrilled about being in the mountains in the middle of nowhere, but I hope she sees that for now, she ain't got no choice."

Reggie came over to the table and took a seat with us.

"I don't like to say this, guys, but I'm thinking we need to lock her down. I mean, I know she's technically a client, but we can't risk another fuckup like this. It's one thing, her putting her own life in danger. But if we're expected to go after her, then our lives are in danger, too."

"Well, if she splits again, I suppose we could just let her go," Jack suggested.

Reggie shook his head adamantly. "No, man. That is

not an option. That's not what Morrow asked us to do. He charged us with her safety."

Jack nodded slowly. "You're right. It's not what her old man would want us to do, either. I mean, I knew Erickson. He'd want us to keep his daughter safe at *all* costs."

Reggie got up and went back to stirring the pot on the stove. "Guess we know what we have to do, then."

"What's that? What do we have to do?" Phee asked, surprising us by appearing in the dining room.

Jack and I looked at each other. Christ, she was fucking gorgeous and, now that she'd had a little rest, downright delicious. Not really dressed for the mountains in her long gauze dress and clunky platforms, but one thing at a time.

I needed to get to the point. "Phee, we're very lucky things worked out today in our favor. But they might not have. Because of that, we can't risk your running off again."

"I don't blame you." She hung her head. "I want to say I'm sorry, but I don't think an apology would cut it, to be honest." She nervously picked at her cuticles, frowning at her chipped manicure. "I know... I know I messed up badly today. I'm so sorry."

"We appreciate your acknowledging that, Phee," Jack said. "But from here on out, we'll have to keep a closer eye on you."

She nodded slowly. "What does that mean?"

"For one, we'll be keeping all our car keys someplace secure. And we'll also be locking you in your room at night."

Her face fell. "What? Are you kidding? I just apologized. I'm not going to pull something like this again."

"Phee, you've got to understand that not only did you put yourself in danger, you also put the rest of us in danger. We don't take unnecessary risks," he added.

She looked around at the three of us, just as Axel entered the room wearing his weight belt and pouring sweat.

He stopped short. "Why is everyone staring at me? You look like someone died."

"Someone *did* die, Axe," Reggie called from the kitchen. "You shot them, remember?"

Axel held his hands up like a *stop* sign.

"You know what I meant. What's going on?" he asked, wiping his brow with a ratty towel.

"We were just explaining to Phee some of the restrictions we need to put on her," I said.

"Oh yeah, no more fuckups, if you don't mind," he said before heading for the shower. "Shooting people is not how I like to spend my days."

That was Axel. Never one to mince words.

"But—" Phee called after him.

He whipped around, his icy eyes and clenched jaw saying what words didn't need to. She dropped whatever she was going to say.

"Join us, Phee," Jack said. "Let me pour you some red. See, you're not being completely deprived. We actually have a very nice wine collection. And whatever rules we need to impose on you are for your benefit. No one else's. This is not jail."

She hesitated, as if she couldn't decide whether to be pissed at us or not. But then, she shrugged and pulled out a chair.

Dinner was fantastic, as it always was when Reggie was chef. Actually, we were all pretty good cooks, and we had a competition thing going on where we kept raising the bar. I had to admit, we were known to binge-watch the Cooking Channel and then come up with ways to outdo each other.

Hey, there were worse ways to spend one's time.

The wine Reggie had paired with dinner was kick-ass, too. Phee especially enjoyed it.

Actually, she enjoyed it a bit too much.

"Ya know, you guys didn't need to *shoot* Sammy," she slurred after her third—or was it her fifth?—glass.

"Really, Phee? And why is that?" Axel asked. He always had to be the instigator. It was in his blood.

"He was a *nice* guy, Axel," she said, slamming her hand on the dining table. "And I really wanted to have *sex* with him. Now he's dead."

Wow. She didn't put out? Or was he the one holding out?

I moved her plate out of the way before it landed on the floor.

"Phee, do ya think it might be time for you to go to bed?" Axel asked, rolling his eyes.

She leaned back in her chair and crossed her arms. "Why don't you just *shut up*, Axel?"

Jack popped up from his chair. "Okay, dinner's over, everyone. Axe, why don't you help me clear the table?"

He sneaked a glance at me.

'Nuff said.

I walked around the table, holding out my arm to Phee. "May I escort you to your room, ma'am?" I asked as gallantly as possible.

The frown on her face turned to delight.

I had a feeling that would soothe her.

"Of course. Thank you, *Spence*," she said, throwing a dirty look over her shoulder at Axel.

Note to self: keep those two away from each other.

The next morning, as I was heading down for breakfast, I heard a quiet *tap, tap, tap* coming from the inside of Phee's bedroom door.

"Phee, good morning!" I called, unlocking it.

She opened it cautiously and peered out. "Hi, Spence," she croaked, eyes bleary and half squinting. "Am I alive?"

"Need some aspirin, I see. I seem to remember you really enjoyed your wine last night," I said.

"Yeah. I guess I did," she admitted, stretching.

Cripes, even with a hangover, she still managed to be a stunner in a little pink nightie and bare feet.

"Oh!" she said, looking behind me.

I turned to find Reggie walking toward us, butt naked, rubbing a bath towel through his wet hair.

"Morning, all," he said cheerfully, continuing past us down the hall.

"Dude, how 'bout some pants?" I called. We were used to his wanderings, but things were different with a woman on the premises.

He turned and gave us a full frontal.

Just what I wanted at eight a.m. But then, I knew he didn't do it for *me*. He did it for his female audience.

"Sorry, guys. I had a little sunrise swim. It was amazing." He turned the corner and was gone.

Phee crossed her arms and leaned on the doorjamb. "Don't tell me. He skinny dips?" she asked.

"Something like that. Hey, want to come down for breakfast, and then I'll show you a nice place for a swim?"

Her face lit up, quite the contrast to her breakdown of the previous day.

"Yeah, that sounds awesome. As long as it doesn't have snapping turtles," she said, mustering a hopeful smile.

"Stick with me and I'll keep you safe from assassins… and snapping turtles."

She laughed. "Oooh, a two-for-one deal. I'll take it."

Not an hour later, we were making our way through the woods to my favorite swimming hole. It was really not much more than a wide spot in a stream running through our property, but that kept it nice and shallow with a sandy little beach on one side and smooth river rocks on the other.

"Wow," Phee said, stopping short. "It's like a little fairy glen in the forest."

"Right? This place is killer." I threw my towel down on the ground and started to strip.

She was pulling off her T-shirt and shorts to reveal a tight little bikini when she noticed I was naked.

"Oh. Gosh," she said, blushing and looking away. "Did you forget your bathing suit, Spence? I can wait while you go back up to the house."

In the meantime, she stood there in a little blue number that barely covered her... assets.

Which meant that if I didn't get in the cool water right away, I'd be sporting some serious wood.

I didn't have a swimsuit, anyway.

She thought all she had to worry about were assassins and snapping turtles?

"The water's great," I yelled, ignoring her comment and running until I was up to my chest. "Come on in!"

"One sec," she called, taking a moment to tie her hair into cute, messy cluster on top of her head. Guess she realized I was *not* going back to the house for a bathing suit.

She wriggled her toes in the water, giving me the chance to admire her curvy hips and perky little breasts... and hope my hard cock would go back down to size before I scared the shit out of her.

She waded in a little further, and when she'd decided the water wasn't too cold, she jumped in all the way, bouncing up and down in delight.

And bouncing those cute little tits at the same time.

"This is lovely," she said, looking around.

She was lovely, truth be told, a woodland nymph lighting up the forest around her. The sunlight that made its way through the trees lit up her golden hair. And other things.

"So, what do you think of Savage Mountain so far?" I asked, wading toward her.

She fanned her hands over the water in front of her.

"I can see the beauty in it. I mean, I'm not much of an outdoorsy person, but it's so pretty and peaceful. I can see why you like it. And I think I'm getting used to it."

She tilted her head and looked up at me. "Thank you for all you've done for me the last few days, Spence. I know I put you in danger. That was wrong."

Fuck, I couldn't help myself. I lowered my lips to hers and stole a quick kiss.

"*Oh.*" Her hand flew to her mouth, and she ran her fingers over her lips.

I backed up in the water. "Sorry, Phee. I shouldn't have done that."

Actually, I was very glad I had. And now, the ball was in her court.

She gave me a small smile and took a step toward me, sucking in a deep breath and pulling her shoulders back. "Why are you sorry?" She ran her hand through my soaked beard.

Well, that was all the encouragement I needed. I scooped my arms around her and pulled her close, my lips running up and down her damp neck while she dug her nails into my bare ass. I was afraid my erection might scare her off, but she knowingly rubbed against it with a barely perceptible moan.

Damn. Who knew?

In one swift motion, I lifted her out of the water and brought her to my beach towel. I kissed her again deeply, our tongues exploring, and then moved down to the little triangles of fabric covering her nipples. I slipped the blue material aside and tasted her. She responded by arching into me, begging for more.

But I had other plans, and I wandered down her taut stomach past her perfect belly button. When I reached the triangle covering her pussy, I kissed her through the thin fabric, and when she moaned, I knew she was ready for more.

Slipping aside the tiny swatch, I found her bare lips soaked with excitement. I ran my tongue through them, and she bucked, pounding her fists into the sand under our beach blanket.

I untied the strings holding the scrap of fabric around her hips and buried my face between her legs. With my other hand, I fisted my hard cock, stroking it carefully to avoid shooting my wad all over the place. It had been a while since I'd been with any woman, much less one this beautiful.

"Spence, I'm coming, I'm coming," she breathed, her head lolling back and forth.

I flicked my tongue faster on her clit, and she exploded in an orgasm that ran her over like a freight train.

My balls tightened, and I could feel my own explosion coming. Moving so I could press my cock to her tits, I came all over them.

She might be rich. She might be spoiled. But she was fucking sexy as hell and wasn't afraid to have a good time.

My kind of girl.

CHAPTER 7

PHEE

India shrieked at me over the phone. "Phee, where have you been, and why haven't you been returning my calls?"

"I'm sorry. I have bad cell coverage here," I semi-lied.

Yeah, the mountain didn't always get the best coverage but that wasn't the reason I hadn't called. Truth was, I'd been avoiding talking to her. After what went down with Sammy, I needed time to clear my head.

India deserved to know what had happened to him, of course—he was her friend, too. But I wasn't ready to share the sordid story. It had been beyond traumatic, and I was still reeling. I'd seen him bleeding on the tarmac. Actually, I'd seen him dead.

And I'd thought the bastard cared about me.

She gave a long, drawn-out sigh. "Fine. Hey, I wanted to tell you that no one has seen or heard from Sammy in several days. His car is in his driveway, but he's nowhere to be found."

My stomach dropped. Of course India was going to bring him up, wondering where the hell he was.

But it was nevertheless unnerving to hear her say his name, like he was still a good guy. Still part of our circle of friends.

I fought to stave off the dizziness that was making me queasy. "What? What do you mean, he's missing? Where could he have gone?" I asked, forcing myself to sound both concerned and oblivious to the fact that he was probably rotting in a shallow grave somewhere.

I hoped I sounded sufficiently dramatic. It was hard to do when you were trying not to vomit.

She hesitated. "Are you sure you haven't heard from him? I know he was really worried about you, having to leave town so quickly and stuff."

"Nope, not heard a word."

I heard her pacing. "I thought, I mean, he had told me he was going to try to find you. He wanted to keep you safe, safer than anyone else could," she said.

"Oh no. I wonder where he is," I said lamely. I'd never been a good liar.

There was an awkward silence, which I'd never had

before with India. It was like she didn't believe me, and I didn't believe her. Like some sort of standoff.

"Hey, India, the connection's getting bad—"

Another lie.

I swiped my phone closed. Something felt off.

I thought back to when I'd met Sammy. India had been dying to introduce us. In fact, she pushed for weeks until I caved and agreed to meet him.

It had seemed kind of weird how insistent she'd been, but at the time, I hadn't put much stock in it. I'd just thought she really wanted to fix her guy friend up, and I was single and available, so it was a no-brainer.

But Sammy had really worked it, too. From the moment we'd met, he'd laid it on thick. I just figured he hadn't dated anyone in a while. It was nice to have a new guy to hang out with and I was hoping at some point some hot sex might come out of it. Although, he always had a reason to wait a bit longer.

At the time I'd thought it was chivalrous. Now, I wasn't so sure.

Since the crazy airport shootout, I'd racked my brain for signs I might have picked up on, which would have hinted at who Sammy really was. And there *had* been signs. I guess looking back, there always are.

A couple weeks into dating him, India had suggested we get a bunch of people together to go to the Caribbean for a week. She found a house, lined up some friends I didn't know very well, and we were off.

Of course, Sammy came.

No one ever paid me back the money I fronted for

the house. I mean, I figured I'd eventually get reimbursed, but I felt funny bringing it up, and then weeks passed, and I just dropped it. I knew India lived on a tight budget, so I often paid for things. Didn't give it a second thought, actually. Guess I should have. My mother had warned me about people like that, people who take advantage of people like us.

But what was really strange was the afternoon India and Sammy disappeared. They'd gone out to get tequila for margaritas, but they were gone three hours. At the time, I'd been pretty annoyed at being left behind in a house with people I barely knew, but now, I wondered if that was part of a pattern that was, honestly, pretty fucked-up. I couldn't say with any certainty they'd done something inappropriate, but it didn't look good.

So, on top of losing my parents, discovering the guy I was dating was trying to off me, and wondering whether my best friend was up to no good, my life was pretty much in the shitter.

I pulled on my hiking boots, which I still had not managed to break in. I wasn't fooling anyone passing myself off as a mountain girl, but I had to admit, the boots were comfortable and I planned to wear them more. And, I was kind of hoping that would impress the guys.

Oh, the guys. The men of Savage Mountain. I'd never seen such a gorgeous collection of human beings all in one place. Seriously, when god made that crew, he was having a damn good day. Each of them handsome in a different way, and all built like trucks, it was all I could do to keep from drooling every night at the dinner table. Even if they were assholes about locking me in my room at night.

And the sexy time I'd had with Spence at the swimming hole? Yowsa. That was some unforgettable fun. In fact, I was kind of hoping we could go back, maybe for a repeat performance. He was the quintessential burly mountain man with that hulking physique and long scraggly beard.

But that morning when I wandered into the kitchen to grab my breakfast yogurt, everyone was long gone. Where did they go all day? To chop down trees and hunt for food? Who the hell knew?

Luckily, I had a couple of ways to occupy my day. I grabbed my good sketchpad—not the one that had landed in the pond with me—and headed to the watering hole Spence had shown me—the one location on the mountain I could find without getting lost.

When I got to the tiny sand beach, I spread out my towel and stripped down to my bikini. I opened my sketchpad and in minutes was transported a world away as I made long strokes over the page, recreating the idyllic scenery surrounding me, using my own artistic twist.

Naturally, I thought back to the hot session I'd had with Spence right there on the beach. I couldn't believe how sexy it had been that he just dropped trou and wandered right into the water, completely unselfconscious in his perfect nudity. I wasn't sure I could do that.

I'd only ever skinny-dipped once, and that was at summer camp with a bunch of girls. I'd considered doing it in my parents' pool, but the household help was always around, which left privacy in short supply.

But now, at the watering hole, I was alone. I looked around to make sure I had complete solitude, untied my bikini, and ran for the water.

And it was heavenly, floating on the surface with spots of sun hitting me through the canopy of trees. It almost made me forget all that had gone down in recent days.

Almost.

Until I heard someone calling my name. Because, of course.

"Phee! Hey, I didn't know you were down here," Reggie said, standing on the edge of the water.

Shit.

I shrieked and ducked under the surface. But I was pretty sure he'd seen me.

"How's the water?" he called cheerfully, and I remembered that he, too, didn't seem to mind being naked in front of me, just like Spence hadn't.

"Hi, Reggie. Hey, would you mind turning around while I get out of the water?"

On second thought, maybe I should just walk out of the water in front of him and cause him no end of torment. He'd done it to me, after all.

Confusion crossed his face, and he shrugged. "Yeah, sure."

Didn't these guys have any sense of privacy?

Seemed they'd been in the damn mountains way too long.

I dashed out of the water and scooped up my towel off the sand. When I was decently wrapped, I gave him permission to turn around.

He plopped himself on the ground and reached for my sketchpad.

"Whatcha drawing?" he asked, making himself at home with my things.

I snatched it back. I didn't let anyone see my sketches.

"Those are good," Reggie said as I stuffed my belongings in my bag.

I dragged my shorts on under the towel I was wrapped in and pulled my T-shirt over it. In just a few seconds, I was dressed again, without having exposed anything. Score one for women's' ingenuity.

I was pretty impressed with Reggie, too, if I were to be honest about it. He was nearly as buff as Spence and Axel, but leaner. And damn if his salt 'n' pepper hair didn't lend him that devastating silver-fox look. He had a big tattoo on one arm and unlike most men, easily pulled off the funky jewelry he wore.

"What's that necklace you have there?" I asked.

"It's a tribal thing I got during my travels in the Middle East. Just like this silver bracelet I'm wearing."

"Beautiful. Really cool pieces," I said, trying not to stare. I looked over his shoulder and pointed. "Hey, what's that path over there?"

He followed my gaze, hesitating for a moment.

"That… goes… well, it's hard to explain. I'll show you."

Why not?

I followed him along the narrow, nearly-overgrown trail, grateful I'd worn my hiking boots and that I'd made a wise decision about *something* in my life.

After a few twists and turns in the hilly path, we came to a rusty old door built into a hillside.

"What is this? Left over from prohibition days?" I laughed. "You guys rum runners or something?"

He pulled a set of keys out of his pocket and inserted one into the door's padlock.

"This isn't nearly that old. In fact, we had it built when we bought the property."

He pushed the door open, but all I could see was darkness, the musty smell reminding me of my parents' basement.

He reached inside and came back with an LED lamp that he switched on. "Here. This should help."

Holy shit.

I stood before a room outfitted like a studio apartment with bunk beds, desks, and even computers. Enough for four guys to live in. A dude sort of clubhouse, if you wanted to be really descriptive. Or a *man cave*.

"What *is* this place?" I asked, peering into the dim room.

He entered and turned on another battery-powered light. "This is our fallback bunker. Powered by generators."

I bit my lip to keep from laughing. "You have a bunker? Are you guys survivalists, waiting for the 'man' to come up and steal your freedom or something?"

He smiled. "Not exactly. Like your dad, we've all done some… interesting work over the years, and we need to be prepared at all times for anything that might happen. We come down here about once a month or so to make sure everything's in working order, clean a bit. Stuff like that"

He turned out the lights and started to lock up.

"Wait," I said. "Can I take a look?"

"Sure. Be my guest." He pushed the door back open.

A cool wave of underground air hit me, like entering a cellar on a hot summer day. But it was cozy in a non-basement sort of way with rugs all over the floor, nice quilts on the beds, and even a shelf of books.

I walked around, incredulous. "This is insane."

I found Reggie staring at me, and in spite of the cool air in the bunker, a wave of heat washed over me.

"You know what's insane?" he asked, walking toward me. "How beautiful you are."

His words were simple… clear… and utterly electrifying. He reached for the nape of my neck and released my hair from the clip holding it. Pushing the stray pieces away from my face, he closed his fist around a big chunk and yanked my head back.

It didn't hurt. The funny thing was, it was hot. Hot as hell. I barely knew the guy, and that somehow made his self-assuredness even hotter—like he knew something about me that I didn't.

"So pretty," he murmured, running his lips down my bare neck and covering me in goose bumps.

Cripes, this guy was hot, and after the shit that had been going down in my life, he was just what I needed—someone to make me feel good. Someone to make me forget. Like Spence had after swimming.

Messing around with two guys who were friends? Might not be cool, but I hoped there'd be no drama. I'd be out of there in a few days and never see any of them again.

So I decided to go for it.

I took his hand and led him to an armchair where I sat and had him stand right in front of me.

I looked up at him, and our gazes locked while I unzipped his fly and released a very hard cock from restrictive blue jeans. I slid my hand up and down his shaft, and his eyes fell closed.

"Fuck, that feels nice," he said, leaning his hips toward me for more. "Been too long… mmmm."

God, if he wasn't a beautiful man with black-and-gray stubble in the beard lightly covering his chiseled jaw. He ripped off his T-shirt and threw it aside, and then, he grabbed the base of his cock to hold it for me.

His tip glistened with a first drop of precum. I placed my lips over his swollen head, just encasing the rim, and ran my tongue over his sensitive flesh.

"Jesus Christ!" he gasped. "Baby, you're gonna make me blow."

I placed one hand on his ass, digging my nails into

his cheek to pull him to me, and the other cradled his balls, which were already hard and tight.

Then, I took him all the way. He bumped the back of my throat, and I withdrew him again. One look, and I knew I had him.

He tangled his fingers in my hair and rammed his dick in my mouth again, bumping my throat over and over. My attempts not to gag were futile, and tears streamed from my eyes and saliva down my chin.

But I loved it. I loved how he was fucking my hungry mouth.

With a primal roar, he thrust deep into my throat one more time, and my mouth flooded with his hot semen, sweet and salty, powerful and beautiful.

I sucked him clean while he watched, and then he walked me over to one of the beds where he began to undress me.

He was still hard and ready for round two.

CHAPTER 8

REGGIE

I whipped around a corner on the narrow road that led down Savage Mountain just in time to slam on the brakes with all the strength in my right leg. Fortunately, good reflexes and anti-lock brakes stopped my truck just before it slammed into a momma deer and her two spotted fawns.

I glanced next to me where Phee sat in the passenger seat, her mouth open and eyes wide, seatbelt locked and pressing into her chest. I don't know who was more scared, she or the animals I'd narrowly missed.

The momma deer gave us the stink eye and ran into the forest with her two babies right on her heels.

"Holy shit, that was close, Reggie." Phee held her hand against her chest as if to still her pounding heart.

I couldn't lie. My heart was about to jump out of its rib cage, too.

"Christ, it sure was. But to be honest, it happens all the time," I said, putting the truck back in gear and continuing our descent.

"Whew. I guess it does in a place like this. How long have you lived here, anyway?" she asked, looking at me with her brown eyes, blonde hair whipping in the open window.

"Long time," I admit. "I was the first one up here."

"Where were you before the mountain?"

I knew those sorts of questions would eventually come. But Phee was practically family, so I felt free to tell my own story.

"I was in the Army. Grew up poor and enlisted young to get out of a bad neighborhood. Never knew my dad, and my mom couldn't have given two shits about me."

She nodded. I knew her life couldn't have been more different from mine, but I didn't see any pity or judgment crossing her face. I liked that.

"Was the military a good move for you?" she asked with sincere interest.

I nodded. "It was. It got me through college, then special ops, and then the private sector, which turned out to be very lucrative. I was able to retire early."

She held on tightly as we went through a couple

potholes. "So, you're not in touch with any family, Reggie?"

I wish I could say I wasn't. I'd rather be left the hell alone.

"When my mom realized I was making big money—private security companies pay extremely well—she started coming around. Acting real friendly and all."

I tried not to sound bitter, but it felt good to talk about this shit. It had been a long time since I'd had any female company, and a *really* long time since I'd had Phee's sort of female company.

I took her hand, her warm fingers disappearing in my large paw. She might come off as a sheltered rich girl, but she was open to new experiences, and that's what made life worth living.

"And you, what do you do with your free time? When you're not on Savage Mountain, that is."

She sighed. "I do a variety of activities. I volunteer. I like to study languages." She glanced at me. "And of course, I draw and paint. I'm working on an art book, in fact," she said, proudly.

"No kidding. About what, exactly?"

"Well, have you heard of Picasso?"

I laughed. "Of course."

"He was part of an art movement called 'cubism.' I want to write a book about that."

"Awesome. Are you gonna work on it while you're here? On the mountain?"

She shrugged. "I might give it a try. I haven't felt that motivated, what with everything going on…"

I squeezed her fingers. "I don't know if anyone told you, but I knew your father. Not as well as Jack, but I knew him and had a lot of respect for him."

She looked down at her lap, and in her profile, I could see a couple tears roll down her face.

"Oh shit. Sorry. Shouldn't have brought it up," I said.

What a numbskull I was.

Sniffling, she said, "No, it's okay, Reggie. It's good to hear people talk about him. Makes me feel closer to him. It's sad. It always will be. But that doesn't mean I don't want to hear about him or think about him. He was a good dad. And I had a good mom, too. I wish I'd been a better daughter."

I watched her look out the window with a face full of regret. But didn't we all have regrets? I mean, they were inevitable.

"In what way do you wish you'd been better?"

She shrugged. "I could have spent more time with them. Done more for them. Listened more closely when I had the chance."

I hated to see her suffering, but I knew that was part of grief. And there was no way around it. To get to the other side, you have to swim right through it. There were no shortcuts to take.

Phee's face brightened when we pulled into town, which was actually not much more than a village.

"Check out this place. It's cute," she said, looking around as I turned onto Main Street.

I parked the truck in front of the local art store,

which seemed remarkably well stocked for the size of the town. I attributed that to the nearby university, as well as the fine arts retreats held on campus every summer. We guys might be sequestered up on the mountain, but that didn't mean we didn't know what was going on in the outside world.

I followed Phee around the store while she filled a basket with art supplies, and pretty soon, I was carrying that basket and she was stuffing another.

"Hey, calm down. We can always come back if you want," I said as she piled in more items.

She looked at the two baskets between us and then up at me with her luscious smile. "You're right. I *am* going overboard. But having this stuff is a sort of comfort. You know what I mean?"

I did know what she meant. It was funny, the things that brought us a sense of well being when we were out of our element. I had a small book of poetry that had been my grandfather's, which I'd carried on all my missions, and which now lived on my nightstand next to my bed. It didn't cost me anything, and it wasn't much to look at, but having it close by had always been a kind of security blanket.

Phee threw four more sketchpads of varying sizes into the basket I was carrying, and we headed for the checkout, where she pulled out a huge wad of cash from her bag.

She saw me staring. "Oh, Morrow got me a bunch of cash. He didn't want me using credit cards or anything that could be tracked."

Smart.

When we got outside, laden with packages, she asked, "Hey, do you mind if we pop in that outdoors shop over there? I'd like to get a couple things."

"*You* want outdoor clothing? You, Phee Erickson?"

She slapped me on the arm. "Hey, I'm adapting. I like the feel of that fleece jacket you're wearing. Very cozy. I'd like one." She ran her hand up and down my sleeve, and my dick twitched just enough to remind me of our time in the bunker the previous day.

Like I could ever forget that.

We crossed the street and entered a store decorated with hunting wallpaper and the heads of dead stuffed animals.

"Hi," Phee said to the clerk behind the counter. "I'd like to see some fleece jackets, maybe a vest, and a couple flannel shirts. Plaid of course."

She looked at me proudly and I couldn't help but smile back.

I couldn't wait to see her in flannel. And hopefully nothing else.

The clerk, a pimply teenage boy, nearly fell over when Phee spoke to him. Not many girls in high school looked like her, I reckoned.

"Um, yes, ma'am. Let me get my boss to help you. He's really good at picking out stuff."

Phee was entirely oblivious to the effect she had on the kid, but I got a kick out of it. I stood back to watch the show.

A guy with a crooked porn star moustache and too-tight Wranglers appeared from the back of the store wearing an annoyed expression—that is, until he got a look at Phee, whom he checked out from head to toe without an ounce of discretion. We'd probably interrupted him watching internet porn.

Douche.

"Hello, ma'am. Steve here tells me you'd like some assistance," he said, puffing his chest up and sucking his stomach in.

Phee whirled around from the rack she was picking through and smiled. "Yes. That would be great."

He just stared at her, lost for words.

"I'm sorry," Phee said to him, trying to snap him out of his trance, "are you okay?"

I was enjoying this too much. She had him wrapped around her little finger without even trying.

"I think a lovely lady like you should try a couple shirts like this, and here—do you like this jacket?" he asked.

He held up a fleece for her to try on, and when she did, he actually started to zip it for her.

She giggled politely. "I've got it, thanks."

She turned in front of the three-way mirror as the manager drooled over her and the teenage boy watched from his station at the cash register.

"Um, are you new in town?"

She glanced at me. "Yes. I mean, no. I'm just passing through."

She tried on a down vest, and nodded, adding it to what she called her 'yes pile.' She threw three plaid flannel shirts and a couple of fleeces into the mix and was ready to go.

"I think I'm all set."

He nodded, assuming a strange formality.

Dude, this wasn't Saks Fifth Avenue.

"Please come with me to the register."

Nudging the teenager out of the way, the manager leaned toward Phee as he rang her items. "Well, I'd love to show you around sometime. Take you up the mountain, something fun like that."

She smiled politely. "Oh, thank you. But I'm not available for something like that."

I had to hand it to her—that was a nice way to let a guy down.

But he didn't get the hint.

"You really should join me. I grew up here and know all the best places." He handed her a big shopping bag and ran a finger up her bare arm.

"Excuse me," she said, moving out of his reach.

He turned back to the register but not before mumbling, "*Whatever*, bitch."

Okay. That was too much.

"Excuse me," I said, leaning over the counter.

The guy, who previously had not paid any attention to me, turned my way, frowning with irritation. But when he looked up at me, he forced a painful smile.

"Oh. Hello," he said, taking a step back.

"The woman said *no*. Do you know what *no* means?" I asked.

He swallowed and nodded. "Yeah. Yes. Sorry." He

turned on his heel and headed to the back of the store. I looked at the kid behind the counter, who quickly busied himself with stacking hangers or some such.

I guessed shit like that happened to women all the time, because Phee was unfazed.

We left the store, and back in the sunshine, she sang, "I got me some new mountain duds." She shimmied her shoulders with pride.

I'd surprised myself when I told the creepy manager to back off. I wasn't normally a jealous guy. But there was something about Phee and how she'd been going through a bunch of shit, but with the bravest possible face, that made me feel protective.

I could get used to hanging out with a woman like her.

Actually, I already was.

CHAPTER 9

PHEE

"**H**eard all about your little escape attempt," Morrow said when I called him to check in.

Oh, I knew that tone. I'd never met anyone who could somehow sound like he was being critical while being an 'employee' at the same time.

"Yeah, it was a bad scene. I messed up, Morrow. I should never have tried to leave or trust that creep. But how was I to know?" I asked, plopping down on a chair on the house's front porch.

He sighed. "That's the point, Phee. You *shouldn't* know. It's simply not possible. That's why I asked you to lay low until I could do some recon. We would have found out who Sammy was if you'd told us about him. You put a lot of lives at risk by running off like that."

He was right, and my stomach roiled as I thought about how awful it would have been if something had happened to any of the guys, even Axel, the grade A grump who rarely had more than two words for me.

Not to mention how fucking hot he was with all those piercings.

Down, girl.

"I know, Morrow. I should not have done that. I feel like I can't trust anyone, now. I mean, I thought Sammy and I were really becoming a couple."

The humiliation made me want to crawl away in shame.

"That's why your dad had me on the payroll. We ran background checks on everyone. You wouldn't believe some of the things we find out about people. If we'd run one on Sammy sooner, your parents might be alive."

And now the fucker was dead. Just like my parents.

"I never knew any of this, what you guys did to keep my family safe. I wished I'd been more curious about my dad's business when he was alive."

Morrow hesitated for a second. "He didn't want to burden you or make you worry, and he wouldn't have shared much, anyway. He was honestly glad you didn't ask too many questions. Too risky. In fact, he was pleased your interests were more toward the arts and languages. He didn't want you following in his footsteps."

A pain pierced my chest, knowing that Morrow had

discussed me with my dad and knew things about him that I didn't.

"But Morrow, at least I could have been supportive of him. When I think of him carrying all those concerns on his shoulders, all alone, it breaks my heart."

I heard footsteps approaching and wiped my tears. "I gotta go, Morrow," I said and swiped my phone closed.

Jack found me on the porch and took a seat next to me. "Heya. How's it going?"

I sniffled, hoping he wouldn't notice. The way he looked at me with those damn baby blue eyes and his thick hair blowing in the breeze made my tears dry right up.

God bless that man.

I tried not to stare. "I'm well. Just checking in with Morrow, my family security guy."

Although, I no longer really had a family.

"I bet he had some advice for you."

"You mean, don't take off with any more guys I'm dating, because they might turn out to be assassins?" I asked.

He laughed. "Yeah. Something like that."

Cripes if he wasn't looking at me like he could really see me. What was it about his stare that unnerved me?

Jack laughed and changed the subject. "Hey, some of us guys are going camping. You can come, if you want."

Was he making fun of me? Because I was pretty sure he was.

"Are you just asking to embarrass me? Because I went to summer camp when I was a kid, you know."

He rolled his eyes. "Hey, I was just extending an invitation. Nothing more. You don't have to read anything into it."

"Well, thank you, but no. I'm hoping to get out of here any day now, as soon as Morrow says it's safe."

I couldn't be certain, but I was pretty sure disappointment crossed his face. Or maybe I was just hoping.

Harsh behavior aside, the guys had been pretty nice to me. Well, with the exception of hard-ass Axel, although god knew I'd tested the patience of them all. But these were temporary digs for me. As soon as I was off Savage Mountain, I'd forget about the guys, and they'd forget about me, too.

Right?

Jack stood from his spot on the swinging chair. "Got stuff to do. See you later."

Crap. I'd offended him. What a shithead I was.

I picked up the new backpack I'd gotten at the outdoors store that now held my art supplies. I felt quite outdoorsy and official as I set off down a path to the swimming hole, the only place I knew to escape to. If I'd been on the mountain longer, I might have made more of an effort to learn my way around, but for the short period I was to be there, I didn't feel the need to go far.

I sat in my familiar place on the slash of sand near the water and removed my hiking boots and new flannel shirt to get some sun on my shoulders. But when I opened my sketchpad, nothing came. I couldn't even drag my drawing pencil across the page. It was like I was paralyzed.

I knew why, too. I now knew I'd be looking over my shoulder the rest of my life. Assessing danger, trying to find a way to survive. Without my dad to do the sort of thinking for me that he had, I'd be dependent on people like Morrow. I was going to be a target just like my parents had been—targeted by scumbags like the ones who stole my parents from me and had almost done me in, too.

I'd spent my whole life in a protective bubble, but now that bubble was popped. Gone. For good. For the first time in days, instead of being overwhelmed with sadness, anger crept up my spine and exploded in me. I threw my sketchpad and pencil to the side and walked into the water, where I picked up some smooth river stones.

"Fuck you!" I screamed and started throwing them at the tree trunks that surrounded me.

I hurled rocks until my arm ached so much, I couldn't lift it up. That's when I waded deeper into the water, fully dressed in my shorts and tank top. I didn't care. I needed the calm water around me before I fully detonated.

All I wanted to do was study languages, draw and paint, and write my little book on art.

Was that so much to ask?

When the afternoon light started to fade, I headed back to the house, long since having dried off in the sun. I knew the guys would eventually wonder where the hell I'd gotten to, and I also knew better than to be out after dark. Just because I now had hiking boots, flannel shirts, and a backpack, that didn't mean I was an outdoorswoman.

But I figured I was faking it pretty well.

Until I heard a noise in the woods.

I stopped in my tracks, frozen with fear, slowly turning to see what it was.

Nothing.

I turned and kept walking, my ears and every other part of my body on high alert.

There it was again. Some sort of rustling.

"Who's there?" I yelled.

Nothing.

So, I started walking faster. Moments later, I heard it again.

Okay. Enough messing around.

I pulled my pack tight on my shoulders and began to run. I sprinted like I hadn't in years, until my lungs were exploding, begging for more air.

I reached the front of the house and doubled over to catch my breath, glancing behind myself repeatedly.

Still nothing.

But I did hear voices from inside the house, and one of them said my name.

I crept toward the kitchen window, staying out of view.

"Axe, she's hot as fuck. What are you talking about?" Spence asked.

Dishes rattled in preparation for dinner.

"Hot has nothing to do with it. She's a pain in the ass and doesn't lift a finger around the house," Axel said.

What? Did he really just say that about *me*?

I mean, in one sense, he was right. I didn't pitch in around the house. I didn't know it was expected of me. I did make my bed, though. And I'd done my own laundry just the other day. I could do things.

Assholes.

I barged in through the front door and headed straight across the courtyard to my room, not stopping to acknowledge the guys.

I dialed India, even though I wasn't feeling good about her. I was desperate for a friend and certainly couldn't unload on the guys. I didn't know what else to do, even if I shouldn't have been speaking with her.

"Phee!" India exclaimed. "I was just thinking about you."

I sighed. "I was thinking about you, too. Ugh. Can't wait to get out of here."

She paused. "Well, when are you leaving? Where will you go? Because I can't wait to see you again."

"I don't know. Morrow is working on things. I'm getting tired of this—"

Morrow's words *be careful* came floating back to me.

So, I just shut my mouth.

"Just tell me where you are, sweetie. I'll come get you," India said.

I quietly pushed my bedroom door closed. "Um, India, don't you have to work or something?"

I heard footsteps in the background.

"India, is someone else there at your place?"

"Huh? Oh, no. Nope. And I can take time off work. Just tell me where you are. I'll leave right away."

What? India never offered to do things for other people.

"Phee? Are you there? C'mon, tell me where you are."

One of the guys hollered that dinner was ready.

"Hey, India, I gotta go—"

"Wait, Phee. Tell me where you are. Serious. I'll come get you—"

I swiped my phone closed without a goodbye.

CHAPTER 10

JACK

"Hey, Phee, make yourself a plate."

"Thanks, Jack. I'm starving."

I watched our beautiful guest enter the dining room. She was damn hot in her new 'mountain clothes,' as she called them.

She went into the kitchen and made herself a plate while the rest of the guys and I waited for her to take a seat. Then, instead of joining us at the table, she poured herself a glass of wine and began to take everything back to her room.

But not before she gave us all a piece of her mind.

She frowned. "I heard you guys talking about me earlier today. That I'm a pain and don't pull my weight around here. Maybe you're right, but I do my best to be pleasant, which is more than I can say for some of you. I know I don't exactly fit in, and there's not much I can do about that."

Oops. Axel could really be a dick sometimes.

"So, you all can kiss my ass. I'll stay out of your way as best I can for the short time I'm here. And when I'm gone, you'll never hear from me again."

Her voice cracked, and she hustled off to her room.

"I didn't mean for her to hear me," Axel said when she was out of earshot.

"Then maybe you shouldn't talk trash about people," Reggie snapped.

We all looked at our plates for a moment. I mean, it was true, Phee didn't do much around the house, but I didn't think we really expected her to. She was a short-timer. It hadn't occurred to me to put her in the rotation for chores.

So yeah, Axel was out of line.

He was always out of line. That's what bitterness will do to you.

I took a couple bites of the steak he had cooked for dinner—say what you want about him, but the asshole could cook—and excused myself to pay a visit to our guest.

"Phee? It's me, Jack," I said, knocking on her bedroom door.

Silence, except for the sound of a fork on a plate.

"Phee, I know you're in there. I can hear you."

I heard her set her plate down. "Come in," she said in a dull voice.

I opened the door to watch her take a sip of wine, looking out her window to avoid my eyes.

I took a seat on the edge of her bed since her room had only one chair. "Hey, you want to go for a walk or something?"

She shook her head and ate another bite of her dinner. "I'm good, thanks. I'll probably go to bed early tonight."

She looked so vulnerable and forlorn. I could have booted Axel's ass for kicking her when she was down, even if it was unintentional.

My mother always said not to say anything behind someone's back that you wouldn't say to their face. I might share that with Axel and see if maybe he could be more thoughtful with his words.

But to see the lovely Phee slumped over her dinner plate, as beautiful as she was sad, gave me a huge gut punch.

"I'm sorry you overheard Axel talking about you. He's a big-mouthed jerk. You should just ignore him."

She sighed. "Whatever. I'll be out of here soon."

Maybe it would be better if she *did* leave. I mean, I'd hate to say goodbye to such a cool chick, but my attachment to her was getting a bit… uncomfortable.

"I know it might not seem like it, Phee, but we actually like having you here. It's been a breath of fresh air. You're a cool girl," I said.

She turned and looked at me where I sat on the bed, giving me a small smile. "Thanks."

I examined her room, which was pretty clean with

the exception of the obscene amount of luggage piled in one corner. Yup, I recalled carrying that shit the first day she'd arrived.

"Hey," I said, gesturing, "can I see your sketchpad? And I heard you're studying and working on a book about art. Are you wanting to teach, someday?" I asked, hoping to draw her out.

Her face brightened at the chance to talk about something pleasant. "Yeah. I wouldn't mind teaching art to children."

"Teaching is wonderful. I really kind of miss it and wonder if it was a mistake to leave academia."

She tilted her head. "Really? You were a teacher? I thought you liked the CIA and all that spy stuff." She laughed, those eyes grabbing me until I couldn't look away. God, I wanted to kiss her…

"I did like my work teaching political science. I mean, it was how I met your dad. And the private sector money was great, don't get me wrong. But there's something about being in the classroom with people eager to learn. There's nothing like it."

She knew exactly what I was talking about and nodded excitedly. "You should see art classes with little kids. They get totally lost in the process. You've never seen a five- or six-year-old focus for so long as when they've been given some tubes of paint, brushes, and newsprint paper. It's the cutest thing, and they're so proud of their work. There's no self-consciousness like there is with adults. No apologies for doing a crappy job. Just pure joy."

Like the joy I was feeling just looking at her.

She reminded me of a girl Axel and I fell for in college. She liked us both, so we had a happy little ménage going. In the end, she fell hard for Axel, leaving me in the dust. But it was all good. They stayed together for years and eventually married.

The unfortunate thing was that the very private sector job she'd pushed him into, in order to start raking in the bucks, was what eventually drove them apart.

Guess all the money in the world doesn't matter when you're alone more than with your partner.

"I tell you what," I said, leaning on my knees, "how about I take you tomorrow to this beautiful place where you can sketch? It's a wide-open field. I think you'll love it."

She perked up. "But I thought you were going camping."

"Not 'til later in the week. You can set up your art supplies, and I'll bring a book to read. I may bring my own sketchpad."

Her gaze snapped in my direction.

"You draw?" she asked, incredulous.

"Yeah. In fact, I might draw you."

Maybe I could even get her to take her clothes off…

She laughed. "We'll see about that. My modeling fees are very high."

That was okay. She'd be worth every penny.

PHEE

Jack hadn't been kidding when he said he knew a kick-ass place for me to do some sketching. I mean, I felt like I was in the middle of *The Sound of Music* or something. As far as the eye could see, there were rolling green hills and mountains just beyond. Who knew such a paradise existed within a twenty-minute walk from the guys' cabin?

"What is this place?" I asked, doing a three-hundred-sixty-degree turn to take it all in.

Jack shrugged, his thumbs hooked in his pockets. "Not sure what it's called. I just think of it as the valley."

"Wow. Just wow."

He shifted the backpack containing my art supplies,

which he had insisted on carrying. "Let me show you my favorite spot," he said, reaching for my hand. "It's just over here."

I loved traipsing along with this man who, in his cargo pants and fitted black T-shirt, had some of the most rad tattoos I'd ever seen. And yet, underneath his take-charge masculinity, he was also kind of bookish. I guess that was to be expected of a former professor.

And that was pretty much how I saw myself, too—sometimes, I loved nothing more than to hide in a corner with a good book. But most people who knew me would never suspect that. In my life *before*—before the sky fell in—people really knew only the side of me that wore expensive couture clothing and flew to Ibiza for the weekend in my father's private jet, where I'd dance on the bar if I'd had enough shots. Where it was a bad day if I was forced to buy something off the rack at the humble Barney's or Neiman's instead of directly from a designer *atelier*.

Yeah, I was pretty sure that part of my life was over.

I grabbed the hand Jack extended, and we found a spot with huge boulders that served as protection from the wind, and a vista where you could see for miles.

"Holy shit." I grabbed my sketchpad and pencils like a greedy little animal. "Oh, my god, I've needed inspiration like this for so long."

Although, staring at Jack's ass during our hike had been pretty darn inspiring.

I crawled onto the highest rock for the best vantage

point thanks to help from my badass hiking boots. Jack settled down on a rock somewhere behind me, where he pulled out his own pad and started to sketch.

After a half hour or so, I climbed down for a drink of water.

"Things good?" he asked, tilting his pad out of my view.

Shy artist. I did the same thing with my finished—and unfinished—work.

"Mmmm," I said, gulping water and wiping my mouth with the back of my hand. Quite the outdoorswoman I was becoming. "What are you drawing?"

"Can't show you. I mean, if you won't show me, I won't show you."

I grabbed for his pad, which he pulled out of my reach with a smirk.

"I tell you what. If you let me sketch you, I'll let you see it," he said, his gorgeous baby blues looking me up and down.

Cripes, if he kept that up, he'd be sketching me stark naked—which sounded kind of awesome, come to think of it.

"All right." I took a seat on a rock opposite him, put my hands on my knees, and smiled.

"Oh no," he said. "That doesn't work for me. I want something more… interesting."

What the hell did that mean?

I leaned so I was sitting on one hip with my legs tucked under.

"That's better," he said, looking me right in the eye.

But he still didn't start drawing.

"Jack, doesn't this work? Is something wrong with how I'm posing?"

If I didn't know better, I'd swear his eyes got darker. "Take off your top."

I looked around. "Really? Out here?"

"Why not?" he asked.

He had a point. We were in the middle of nowhere. So, I pulled my T-shirt off and tossed it aside, followed by my sports bra. The fresh air whispered over my bare chest, and my nipples jumped to attention, the sun sending a wave of relaxing warmth through me.

"That's more like it." Jack glanced between his pad and me and back. "A half-naked woman in the most beautiful place on Earth. Doesn't get any better."

After sketching for a few minutes, he set his pad down. "Actually, it does get better."

He stood from his spot and took a couple steps toward me.

"I'd like to kiss you, Phee," he said, placing his hands on the sides of my face.

Yes.

Without waiting, I leaned toward him. Our lips met, and in the sunshine, with the crisp scent of the green hills, my problems slipped away, if only for a moment. God knew I needed a break from them. Jack's warm lips brushed mine as I stayed soft and pliable beneath him. I wanted to forget and to feel protected, and he was just the man to soothe the jagged edges I'd been fighting.

I parted my lips in further invitation, and he tasted me with a leisurely passion, his hand running over my sun-warmed skin before landing on my breast. He kneaded my flesh and zeroed in on my nipple, which he pulled and pinched with teasing fingers.

Shivers shot up and down my spine.

"Harder," I begged. "Pinch me harder."

His thumb and forefinger closed on my small point, and I gasped from the discomfort.

"More," I whispered, my eyes fluttering closed. I was dying for more.

Fingers of pain illuminated every cell in my body, and I couldn't help but moan from the deliciousness of it. I was alive, more than I'd been since finding out about my parents, and I was grateful for that. I reached for Jack and pulled him to me, eager to connect with the man who'd made my heart pound since he first found me drenched and crying in the woods.

"Come on, baby," he said, helping me to my feet.

He brought me to the picnic blanket he'd spread out and laid me down. He removed my boots, then shimmied my pants down, leaving me in nothing but a nude lace thong.

"What about you?" I asked, smiling, looking at him from head to toe.

I wanted me some naked Jack. Who could blame me?

He regarded me with an intense stare, ripping off his T-shirt and throwing his pants and boxers aside. His erect cock bounced against his ripped stomach, and I felt the wetness between my legs seep onto the blanket below.

I didn't know what he was going to do with me, and I didn't care.

"I've been thinking of you naked every night since I first brought you to the house," he murmured, running kisses down the side of my face.

I squirmed under the tension of his touch. "Now that I'm naked, what are you gonna do?"

"I'm going to fuck you," he said simply, looking at me as if for consent.

Instead of responding, I slid my hand inside my thong and touched my hard clit, running a finger through my soaked folds. Removing it, I rubbed my juices over Jack's lips.

"Fuck, baby, now I've really got to taste you," he said, grabbing my thong at the crotch and tearing it away from my skin.

Pushing my legs up to my chest, he buried his face between my thighs. Long strokes of his tongue racked my body with tremors, leaving me thrashing and pounding my fists against the ground below.

With my orgasm building, I grasped his head and pulled him tighter between my legs. This tipped him off, and he zeroed in on my clit. My breath came fast and deep, and my hips bucked into his mouth.

"God, Jack, I'm coming… " I screamed.

He continued as an orgasm rolled over me, leaving me clenching with shudders.

Giving me a chance to catch my breath, he pulled a condom out of his pants pocket and rolled it over his length.

"You ready, baby?" he asked, his expression the most serious I'd ever seen on him.

Still rocking from my orgasm, I couldn't speak, so I just nodded with a small smile.

"Hey, I have an idea." He pulled me up. "Stand here and put your other foot up there," he said, pointing to a rock.

He turned me to face away and bent me forward until I rested my hands on a boulder. His huge palms smoothed over my back, the rough calluses he'd earned from his time on the mountain a coarse massage on my soft skin.

Notching his cock at my opening, he leaned forward to grip my breasts. He pushed inside me partway, his stretch taking away my breath. He waited while I adjusted to his girth, then filled me with more.

"Fuck, baby, you feel so good," he whispered, pulling on my tits.

I reached back between my legs to both feel him slide in and out of my slick pussy and to stroke my clit, which was hanging heavy and sensitive. Another orgasm built, and I pushed back hard against his thrusts, matching his rhythm.

"Oh, god, Jack, I'm coming again," I murmured, my head bucking as I clawed at the rock for purchase.

He groaned at the top of his lungs with his own orgasm, continuing to piston me until he collapsed in exhaustion. He pulled me down to the blanket, laying me gently, so he could push the hair out of my eyes and smooth his fingertips over my flushed skin.

"Jesus. When you grabbed my balls, my head nearly popped off my shoulders, baby." He leaned to put a kiss on my head.

"Hungry?" he asked after a while.

I nodded. "Mmm-hmm."

"Good, 'cause we've got picnic food!"

"Oh, my god, brilliant. I'm starving," I said, smacking his bare ass as he rifled through his backpack.

He set out a chunk of cheese and some bread and lay on his side next to me, propped up on one arm.

I gobbled down a couple bites to curb my insane hunger. "Guess we didn't get much drawing done."

Jack took my free hand and kissed the back of it. Good thing I was lying down because I think I might have fainted.

"No worries. Time is on our side." He flopped onto his back with his hands under his head. He was a picture of a man without a care in the world.

I wanted to be in that place.

"Hey, I kind of think of you as a sort of Superman," I admitted.

He lifted his eyebrow, somewhat confused. "Huh?"

"Well, you were this mild-mannered professor and became a badass CIA operative. You know how

Superman is this nerd in a suit and then turns into a hunky hero, right?"

He burst out laughing. "So, I'm a nerd? Gee, thanks!"

He flipped me onto my stomach and laid a huge smack on my ass.

"Ouch," I squealed, twisting to protect myself by plastering my hand to my behind.

"Well, I gotta admit, I had reservations about leaving academia, but in the end, I made a good living. So, look at me now," he said, gesturing at the amazing view. "Course, money has its downsides."

I turned to face him, running my fingers over his dark tattoos. "It certainly does. You always have in the back of your mind that someone might be using you for your money, rather than really being interested in your friendship."

He nodded. He understood. "Isn't that the truth."

I plopped onto my back and looked up at the clear sky. "Sometimes, I think I'd like to just be a regular girl with a regular job to go to every day."

Just then a screeching electrical sound came out of the side pocket of his backpack.

"Christ, what is that?" I asked, my heart pounding.

He groaned and reached for his pack, returning with a walkie-talkie. "Jack here," he said, sighing. "Whaddya want?"

I wondered if that meant our art picnic would be coming to a quick close.

"Yo, Jack, it's me, Axel. Come back to the house.

Hurry. Reggie is hurt—" The loud crackling stopped, and everything was silent again.

Jack sat up straight. "Axe? Are you there? Axel?" He looked at the walkie-talkie, turned several buttons on it, and still got nothing.

"Let's go."

CHAPTER 12

AXEL

"Easy, Axe!" Reggie hollered, thick drops of perspiration running down his temples. "That hurts like a motherfucker."

Spence and I guided him into the back seat of the Jeep, helping him to lie as flat as possible. I crumpled up an old blanket and stuffed it under his bleeding leg.

"Breathe, brother, breathe," Spence said in a calm voice.

"Guys! Hey! What happened!" Jack yelled, running toward the house with Phee close on his heels. That must have been the fastest mile either of them had ever run.

"Jack's here," Spence said with relief.

While we were all well trained in first aid, Jack had

the most experience. For some reason he liked that sort of thing.

I pressed on the geyser squirting blood from Reggie's leg, where the drill he'd been using had skipped off wood he was working with, sending the bit into his upper thigh.

I didn't know enough about first aid to determine whether it had hit his femoral artery, but from the amount of blood he was losing, it didn't look good.

"Arrrgghhhh!" Reggie screamed from the pressure I put on his wound.

"What the—" Jack stopped short when he saw us all covered in Reggie's blood, now pooling all over the back seat of the car.

"Ugh, dude, I took a drill to the thigh. Look at that fucking blood," Reggie yelled, pounding his fist against the car seat.

For a moment, my buddy Jack looked stunned. Then, his training took over. "Give me the scissors out of your bag, Phee."

She dumped the contents of her pack on the ground and passed Jack the scissors, which he used to cut off Reggie's pant leg.

"Axe, don't let up the pressure," Jack grunted through clenched teeth, his face drawn in intense concentration.

Problem was, I was beginning to feel sick to my stomach. I'd never been good with blood, much less when it was coming out of one of my friends like a goddamn soda fountain.

"Axel, move. Let me," Phee said, pushing me out of the way.

Without a moment's hesitation, she snatched a towel out of my hand, folded it, spread it evenly over the hole the drill had left behind, and applied smooth, even pressure.

In fact, she didn't even flinch and pressed harder, saying, "Get me more clean towels. Now!"

Of course, that didn't feel very good to Reggie, who screamed again. "Goddamn motherfucker that hurts like a bitch. Someone get me a shot of whisky."

"Got it," Spence said, running for the house.

While Phee applied pressure to Reggie's wound, Jack found the artery in his upper thigh and applied pressure there.

"Sorry, bro, don't mean to give you a ball massage," Jack said.

Our patient side-eyed Jack.

And the bleeding slowed. A little.

"It's all good, dude. Stop this hemorrhage and I'll let you lick my balls," Reggie said with a groan.

Phee laughed and relief washed over me. If Reggie was making crude jokes, he was most likely going to be okay.

When Spence returned, I passed Reggie the whiskey. He took a big guzzle straight from the bottle and closed his eyes as the burn took his mind off his leg.

"Phee, where did you learn first aid?" I asked, incredulous.

All the guys were, really.

She shrugged modestly, and that's when I noticed the sunburn on her arms and her inside-out T-shirt. I bet I knew exactly where Jack took her. I was happy for my friend, if not a little envious, too. I wasn't a warm and fuzzy guy—been through too much shit for that—but I cared about my friends. I liked to see them happy.

"Well, Axe, at summer camp as a kid, we had to learn first aid. I was the best in the class," she said, with a wink.

Yeah. Seemed like she was good at quite a few things.

"Spence, the bleeding seems somewhat under control. How 'bout you and I take him to the hospital?" Jack asked.

Spence nodded and got behind the wheel.

"You guys good with staying behind?" Jack asked. "We can't fit everyone in the car if we're to have Reggie lie down in the back seat. Plus, you guys can make us a nice dinner if you get a wild hair."

I nodded. "Go. Hit the road."

Jack jumped in the passenger side of the front seat, and they took off down the mountain, but not before Reggie hollered, "Make me something good or I'll fuck you up!"

I loved that asshole.

"Oh, my god. Look at us. We're covered in blood," Phee said.

Cripes, even though she looked like she'd been at

the scene of an accident, which I guess she pretty much had been, she still managed to look gorgeous.

"Let's get cleaned up," I said. "You even have blood in your hair." I fingered a strand of it.

"Oh, gross," she groaned

I watched her hustle toward the house, her tight little ass jiggling just the slightest bit in her leggings.

"Join me for a glass of wine after," I called to her.

She whipped around, and I saw the cutest smudge of blood on her face. "Yes please!"

She skipped up the steps, and I headed to my own shower.

***

"Whew," she said, joining me in the sunroom thirty minutes later looking damn adorable in her fluffy white robe and dripping wet hair.

Wonder if she needed help drying those tresses.

"How did Reggie hurt himself? In all the panic, I didn't get the story."

I poured her a glass of red. "I guess he was drilling some wood and hit a nail. It sent the drill flying, unfortunately right into his thigh."

She shook her head, wet hair sticking to her shoulders. "He's lucky he had people around him who knew what to do. You can bleed out pretty fast from an injury like that."

Seriously. He was lucky Phee had been there. We all were. Her calm centered us. I mean, was it a pure coincidence that as soon as she came on the scene and got to work, Reggie's bleeding was brought under control?

Would that have happened if I or one of the other guys had kept pressure on his wound?

She took a long sip of her wine and dropped her head back to look out the sunroom's glass roof. "So Axel. Were you in the CIA, like Jack?" she asked.

"No. I went right from special ops to the private sector. Not your dad's firm but another. It was a big improvement over the Army, nicer digs and better pay, but I was away from home so much that one day, when I came home, the wife was gone."

"Holy crap. That must have been awful," she said, nodding, acknowledging my story but not pitying me. I appreciated that. I did not want anyone feeling sorry for me. Ever.

"Well, what really sucked was that she made off with my brother."

I'd never told anyone that part of the story.

What was it about Phee that was so soothing, you felt like you could tell her anything and she wouldn't judge?

"Cripes," she said, shaking her head.

"And then *he* dumped *her*." I needed to shut my big mouth, but the words just kept pouring out. "I had to pick her up and dust her off, she was so devastated."

"Guess that didn't do much for your relationship with your brother."

Didn't even know if the fucker was still alive.

"We'd never been close. But I never saw that coming, either."

She shook her head. "That's up there with the story of my boyfriend, an assassin who took out my parents, and who was trying to get rid of me, as well."

We were quiet as we finished our wine.

She set her empty glass on the table beside her. "Well, it's been a long day. I don't know when the other guys will get back, but I'm sleepy from the hike and the sun. They'll have to fix their own dinner." She laughed.

"Let me walk you to your room, then."

I didn't want to let this woman out of my sight until the last possible moment. I mean, I wasn't one to get attached, especially after what went down with my ex-wife, but this woman did something to me I couldn't put into words. By any measure, she was stunning, but there were lots of beautiful women out there. Phee was different, though—smart and spunky, even in the face of the serious shit swirling around in her life.

I liked that. The other guys had told me to ease up on her and quit being such a dick. I was glad they had. They'd been right.

"Thank you for the wine, Axel," she said when we got to her door. "It was nice to relax and chat."

I ran my finger along her cheek. I couldn't help myself. If she sent me packing, that would be fine, but I was hoping otherwise.

And just as I'd hoped, she turned her face into my hand, kissing my palm.

"I was moved by your story. Thank you for sharing it with me."

I took a chunk of her hair and ran my fingers through it. "It's funny. I don't share it with many people. Actually, I don't share it with anyone." I pulled her hair to my face and took a long inhale.

In turn, she raised her hand to fiddle with my pierced ear plugs. "I wouldn't be here today if you hadn't gotten me out of that mess in the airfield. In fact, I thought I might offer you a kiss in thanks."

Now we're talking.

"Really? Hmmm. I'll have to think about that. I mean, a kiss is hardly equivalent to having saved your life, don't you think?" I teased.

This woman was making my dick hard.

"What do you think would be fair, then, Axel?" she asked, taking my hand and pulling me into her room.

I followed her. "I'll have to think about it."

She laughed lightly. "Well. I have some ideas." She backed me up to the edge of her bed. I sat and she pulled out my cock.

That's *what I'm talking about.* And her hand was fucking magic.

She kneeled before me, moving her head between my legs to hungrily lick the tip of my cock. She then wrapped her lips around my swollen head, creating a suction that nearly sent me through the roof.

"God, Phee, you're killing me," I groaned.

I wove my fingers into her lush hair and with a

good grip, pushed her head all the way down on my cock.

"Fuuuuuck…" I moaned.

Her gaze met mine with her mouth full of dick, and I swear, the lust in her eyes made me even harder. I moved my ass closer to get deeper in her mouth, gagging her. She never looked away.

What a goddamn heady feeling, when a smart, beautiful woman was working hard to make me feel good. I promised myself I'd never forget this feeling and would do everything in my power to make her mine.

She could belong to all us guys. But when she was with *me*, she'd be *mine*.

As I had that final realization of bursting clarity around what I wanted, my balls tightened and pushed an explosion of hot cum into Phee's mouth. She didn't miss a beat and swallowed my entire wad. When she was done, she gave me a big smile.

Yeah, this woman was going to be mine, one way or the other.

CHAPTER 13

PHEE

After my sexy session with Axel, he said good night and locked me in my room.

Really?

The guys still didn't trust me not to take off in the middle of the night?

Although, with the fiasco around my last disappearance and how it endangered more lives than just my own, I guess I couldn't blame them. But shit, they might as well just tie me to my bed.

Which didn't sound half-bad, if I thought about it.

But interestingly, every morning when I woke up, my door was already unlocked. So, there was that.

As I headed down for my morning coffee, I saw Jack and Spence gathering food from the kitchen.

"Morning. What are you guys doing? And how's Reggie's leg?" Their flexing muscles as they bent and stood were so distracting, I poured coffee all over the counter.

"Oh, hey, Phee. I see you cleaned yesterday's blood off," Jack said. "We're gearing up for our camping trip. I might take my sketchpad. Whaddya think?"

Spence rolled his eyes. "Dude, you always take your sketchpad and you never draw anything."

Jack shrugged while he continued packing pillowy little bags into a larger nylon one.

"What is that?" I asked, pointing. "It looks like something from science class."

He laughed. "It kind of is something from science class. It's freeze-dried—" he picked up the package to read the tiny print, "—chili. It probably won't be too bad."

Reggie called out from the dining table, where he'd propped up his injured leg on a chair. "Hey, I'm over here, and my leg hurts like a mofo, thank you for asking. And Jack loves that crap. You should have seen the time he got freeze-dried peanut butter. Worst thing you ever tasted, take my word."

"Oh, you guys shut it. We've got better stuff for this trip, like beef jerky and dried fruit. The peanut butter was just an experiment," Jack said.

"A failed one!" Reggie added.

I had to admit, I loved the way the guys busted on each other.

"Where are you going camping?" I asked, half wondering if I might invite myself along, even though I'd initially turned my nose up at the idea.

Wait a minute… I didn't camp.

"We're going to the next mountain range over. Hike in all day, camp for a couple days, then hike back out. It's gorgeous over there," Spence said.

"Cool. Just you two?"

He nodded. "Usually we try to leave at least one guy at the house here. Since Reg is laid up, Axel agreed to stay with him."

Here goes…

"D… do you have room for one more person?" I smiled so brightly they'd realize they *had* to invite me along. What the hell? It wasn't like I had anything else to do.

Well, you would have thought I asked for a million dollars with the way all activity in the room came to a screeching halt. Even Axel, who'd just joined us, stopped mid-pour over his coffee mug.

What had I done?

Reggie spoke first and for some reason was wearing a shit-eating grin. "Yeah, guys, take Phee. She'll be an awesome backpacker."

I looked from one face to the next, unsure whether Reggie really meant that or if he was mocking me.

Axel just smiled.

Jack nodded like *why not?*

But Spence—my usually cheerful Spence—scowled.

"Eh, you guys don't have to bring me. Maybe another time." I nodded cheerfully.

Seriously. Staying behind with Axel and Reggie was nothing to turn one's nose up at.

"Phee, you should go," Reggie said, a little too enthusiastically. "In fact, you can use my backpack and my gear."

Spence held his hands up. "No offense, Phee, but we were planning on doing a trip probably more rugged than you would be comfortable with. Our next trip might be better."

Jack cut in. "Naw, Spence, she can come. Phee, you'll have to carry all your own gear and pull your weight. But I'm sure you'll be fine. You seem to be in pretty decent shape."

Gee, thanks.

"I do Pilates three times a week," I said to prove my athleticism.

"What the hell is *pee-la-tays*?" Reggie asked.

These guys had clearly been in the mountains too long. "It's a type of exercise class. Kind of like yoga." Best to leave it at that.

I caught Axel and Reggie giving each other a look.

Did that mean I was a disaster in the making? That they thought I'd be a massive fuckup of epic proportion? I didn't know these guys well enough to read between their squiggly lines.

I smelled a challenge, and now, I *really* wanted to go if for no other reason than to show the guys I could do it—that I could camp, and not complain, and even have a good time. Assholes. I'd show them.

"What do ya say, Spence?" Jack asked.

He looked at me and smiled resignedly as he ran his fingers through his beard. "Sure. Why the hell not? I'll add to our food and water supplies."

Not thirty minutes later, the guys had stuffed a large framed backpack with a few of my clothes and everything else I needed for a couple days in the wilderness. That is, they packed what *they* thought I'd need in the wilderness. It seemed that keeping things light was the top priority, so after food, clothing, and gear, there wasn't weight allowance for much more. That meant I could bring one small sketchpad and a couple pencils.

But I did sneak a paperback into my bag when they weren't looking.

A girl's got to have her reading material, right?

I laced up my boots as Reggie remained at the table with a shit-eating grin and his elevated gimpy leg.

"Too bad you can't come, Reg," I said.

God, he was cute with that crazy grin and funky jewelry. Even if he was mocking my outdoors prowess.

"Oh, don't I know it. Hate to miss the party. But I'm sure you'll have fun. Be good to my camping gear, will ya?"

Axel nodded. "Have fun, sweetie. We'll be awaiting your return," he said with a wink.

Of course, I winked back.

Well now. Wasn't I quite the badass? I mean, I'd officially gone from the life of a pampered heiress to one of a woman who could survive in the great outdoors.

Not so fast, sister.

Truth was, I didn't know how to put up a tent or light a fire, much less cook over one. But I was going to learn.

Right?

Jack and Spence hoisted massive packs onto their backs.

Uh-oh. What was I getting into?

"Okay, Phee. This is how you put on one of these packs without wrenching your back." Jack gestured for me to come over.

"Either have someone hold it for you or prop it onto something like this table, here."

I stared at the thing I'd have to carry on my back. "How heavy is that?" I asked.

He studied it, stroking his chin. "I would guess around thirty pounds. We did our best to lighten it for you. Spence and I have all the food to lessen your load."

Thirty pounds? Was he fucking kidding? What would it have been if I was carrying my food, too?

It wasn't too late. I was still in the safety and relative comfort of the cabin. There was food in the fridge, electricity, and hot water. I could change my mind…

And I would have, except I saw Reggie drumming his fingers on the table, like he was doing a countdown to my death march.

Screw it. I was going.

"Okay. Let's do this," I said as Jack propped my pack on the edge of the kitchen counter.

I turned and wove my arms through the large straps. Jack reached down and clipped a wide belt around my waist. So, at this point, the pack was essentially strapped to me but still sitting on the counter.

"Now, take a step forward," he said, standing close by like he was my spotter.

As I did, the weight of the pack shifted from the table to me. I leaned forward a bit for balance and took a couple of steps.

"Hey. This isn't too bad."

He adjusted the straps to my frame and placed two water bottles in the side pockets. "Yeah? Can you handle it?"

"I think so. Feels pretty good." Amazing, actually.

Axel called out from the dining room. "With the weight distributed like that, you should be pretty comfortable."

All four guys—Reggie and Axel at the dining table, and Jack and Spence with their packs on—looked at me.

"I think I'm ready." I threw my arms up in the air as if to prove it.

"All right, Phee. Let's go," Spence said.

"Make us proud, there," Reggie called after me.

We walked in silence for about an hour, and I had to say that, while my pack was kind of heavy, it wasn't too bad. And the guys carried theirs like they were empty.

Figures.

It was hour two that got to be tough.

The thrill of being with the gorgeous Jack and Spence began to dull as I followed them up the mountain's hilly terrain. I was relieved when Jack suggested we take a little rest.

I knew they were actually taking a break for *me* and not themselves. I grabbed a seat on a log, thinking back to how my life had looked only a couple weeks before. No one, and I mean *no one*, would have ever believed I'd be hiking or camping or doing anything else in the mountains. Not India, nor any of my other friends.

I'd not reached out to her in days, not since she last gave me a bad feeling with her insistence we meet. I didn't want to her to know where I was or how I was. The guys, not to mention Morrow, had me sufficiently paranoid. For heaven's sake, I was afraid of my own shadow these days.

I'd lost so much. My parents, my life. Even my identity, if I thought about it. I mean, if I ever did venture back out in public, I'd probably have to wear a wig and use a fake name.

Fuckers.

But I wasn't going to feel sorry for myself.

After all, I was growing. Look at me, wearing freaking hiking boots and a huge pack on my back. And I was living, even if it was temporarily, with four of the most gorgeous men any woman had ever laid eyes on.

And I'd slept with them, too, a secret I'd probably carry to my grave.

"Ready to roll?" Spence asked, as Jack extended me a hand.

"Lost in thought, huh?" he asked.

Lost in something, that was for sure.

CHAPTER 14

SPENCE

I had to hand it to Phee. She busted her ass to keep up with us and handled the weight of her pack with no complaining. I knew the other guys thought she wouldn't make it the first couple of miles, but fuck them. She wasn't the whiny pain-in-the-ass type. She'd always find a way to keep her chin up, even if she was a sheltered rich girl.

Which wasn't easy with all the shit going down in her life.

We walked another half hour or so when I noticed her slowing. Not a good sign since we had a couple more hours' walking ahead of us, but it wasn't surprising, either. She'd never carried a thirty-pound backpack before, much less up and down a mountain. I dropped back to walk with her, letting Jack forge ahead.

"How ya feeling, there?" I asked as soon as the trail was wide enough for us to walk side by side.

"Oh, pretty good," she said, looking up and sniffling. She wiped her eyes with her sleeve.

"You don't look too happy."

She smiled at me with red eyes. "This walking is so meditative. It lets thoughts bubble to the top of your mind. You know, stuff you'd rather push aside for as long as you can. Like losing my parents. Stuff like that."

I ran my hand over her hair. "Funny you say that."

"Why's that?" she asked. "You have stuff on your mind, too?"

I loved how she got to the point.

"Yeah. Just thinking about my ex-wife and baby." I gave her a side-glance, waiting for the inevitable reaction.

And, there it was—her head whipped at me so fast, it must have hurt her neck.

"Wha...?" she said, stopping right on the trail. "You're a *dad*?"

I nodded, looking up at the tree canopy where two birds chased each other. "Yeah. I am. Although, I haven't felt like one in a while. The ex took off with the baby and left the country. I don't know where they are."

After two years, I could still barely say the words, as

if speaking them out loud made it more real than the nightmare they already were.

But the sad reality was, it wasn't a nightmare. It was my goddamn waking, everyday reality.

Phee's eyes were wide. I had her full attention, now.

"Being in special ops is hard on a marriage. My wife and I decided to split, but we were going to live near each other and raise our little girl, Abby. Then, she met a guy from Brazil, and when I didn't agree to her taking Abby there, she disappeared while I was off on a mission."

For a moment, I chafed when I mistook her expression for pity. I think she was actually angry for me, though. I liked that.

"Oh, my god. How devastating. And I guess you've not heard a word?"

God knew *I wished* I'd heard from them. Something, anything, to know they were alive and okay.

"Nope. I've been to Brazil. Even hired a couple private investigators. They've turned up nothing, but I'll eventually find them. You can't hide forever. And when I do find them, I'll get custody of Abby. My ex won't be able to keep her. International parental kidnapping is a violation of federal law."

We started walking again, her warm hand on my arm. "My god. What a thing to live with. I'm so sorry."

"Yeah. Sucks. I met my wife when we were in college. I was something of a football star, and the pros were looking at me. But I sustained an injury that damaged three of the four ligaments in my knee. I tried to come back from it but never fully recovered."

It felt good to talk about some of the shit that had gone down in my life. I mean, we all have our stories— our crosses to bear, right? I know I didn't have it any worse than anyone else walking down the street, and I wasn't one to feel sorry for myself, but it still felt good to share. It had been a long time since I'd had a nice chat with a woman and a *really* long time since I'd met a woman like Phee.

"The football injury was a disappointment, but to be honest, I wasn't sure I'd have made it to the pros, anyway. I've often wondered if it was all meant to work out just the way it did. And then, I was recruited by the Army."

Phee just shook her head. I wasn't surprised. There was really nothing to say after such a big share.

But she did reach for my fingers, and I couldn't help but gobble them up in my huge paw. It was a sweet gesture, and her kindness got me. Turned me on, too, of course.

"I'm glad you came with Jack and me on this trip."

"I am, too. At least, so far," she said, her laugh leaving a twitch between my legs.

After another fifteen minutes of walking in silence, we saw Jack up ahead, waiting. "Hey, guys. Thought you'd never catch up."

The trail we were on opened to a beautiful grassy clearing with a small stream running through it. Jack already had his tent up.

"Thought we'd camp here for the night rather than push for extra miles," he said.

"Sounds good." I dropped my pack to the ground and turned to help Phee take hers off.

Yeah, we were stopping to accommodate her. Which was fine.

"I can't complain about that. My pack was getting heavy." She rolled her shoulders with the weight of the pack removed.

She pulled off her boots and socks and walked down to the stream's edge, stepping gingerly on uneven rocks and dipping a toe in the water. "Oh, my god! That feels amazing." She sloshed around like a happy little kid.

"Phee, I'm gonna put your tent up for you," I said, unhooking it from the bottom of her pack.

"No, I can do it. Really." She ran out of the water as fast as her tender bare feet would let her.

I stopped. "Are you sure? Have you done it before?"

She shrugged. "No. But just before we left, I read the instructions Reggie gave me." She snatched the tent bag from me.

Okay, then.

"Why don't you take this spot over here?" I suggested, pointing to a nice flat area clear of rocks or branches.

"Great. Thank you." She pulled her tent out of its bag, and the neatly packed poles scattered all over the ground. She looked up with a small smile and sat down to open the instruction sheet.

I had to hand it to her for trying.

Jack and I got busy putting up our tents, keeping one eye on Phee.

First, she had her tent upside down. She figured that out when she couldn't find the zippered front. But we didn't say a word.

Then, she had the short poles where the long poles go and vice versa. But she kept at it, biting her lip in the cutest possible way. And giving us a nice peek every time she bent over in her short shorts.

Two hours later, her tent was up, and she was triumphant. It was lopsided, and she'd neglected to insert one pole, so the middle of it dipped, but it was serviceable. As long as no strong winds whipped up, it wasn't going anywhere.

"Look at that," Jack said, standing from where he was setting up our grill. "Phee, you did an awesome job."

I nodded. "Way to go, baby."

Sweaty and slightly out of breath, she beamed. "It looks like crap, but I did it, and it's all mine."

She skipped over and hugged me, so I picked her up and whirled her around. Couldn't help it. And before I put her back down, I pressed my lips to hers. To my delight, she kissed me back with the kind of hunger I was hoping for.

Jack whistled. "Damn. Look at you two. Get a room, guys."

Hands on hips, Phee tilted her head and turned to him. "Feeling jealous over there?"

Fuck yeah. I knew what was coming next.

"I suppose," Jack said, pulling a sad face.

She glanced at me, and I responded with a wink. I wanted my boy taken care of, too.

Sidling over to Jack, she put her hands on the sides of his face and slowly pressed her lips to his. As she stood on her toes, her little khaki shorts hiked up, giving me another nice view of the cheeks of her curvy ass.

Cripes, watching my sexy girl get it on with another guy gave me a huge fucking woody.

My girl. Yup, I'd said it.

While they got busy, I scrambled for my ground cloth and spread it out nice and smooth. I put rocks on each of the corners to hold it down and walked over to where Phee stood plastered to Jack. I pressed myself to her back, and she pushed her hips back, grinding against my hard cock. We now had a little Phee sandwich.

Game on.

She and Jack kept doing their thing while I reached under her shirt for her firm little tits. Her nipples were like rocks and became even more so when I pulled on them. I couldn't get enough of her soft, warm skin and ran my hands down her stomach and into her shorts.

"Mmmm," she moaned.

It came as no surprise that when I reached her sensitive folds, they were slick with excitement. I flicked her clit as a tease, running firm circles over the little nub. Her head dropped back on my chest, and

Jack showered her neck with kisses, pulling off her top and bra to get to her breasts.

"Oh, fuck, Spence," she said, grinding her ass against my hard dick.

I pulled my hand out of her shorts just as Jack unzipped them and dropped them to her ankles. Now completely naked, she kicked them aside and let me lead her to the ground cloth.

I stripped off my own clothes with record speed and plopped down on my back. "Come here," I growled, beckoning her with a finger. "I want you on my face."

She gave me a naughty smile and hovered over me, providing perfect access to her beautiful, juicy pussy. With one knee on either side of my head, she lowered herself until her lips just hovered above my tongue. With one quick lash, I flicked at her clit, and she cried out.

Fuck, it was all I could do to not blow my wad right then. I had to fight to keep my hands off my dick, I wanted to stroke myself so badly.

So, I wrapped my arms around her thighs, pulling her down tightly on my face so I could rock her up and down on my tongue and reach every crevice between her legs. Clit to ass and back again. Just what the doctor ordered.

Jack stood, offering her his cock, which she eagerly lapped. With a quick glance up, I saw his fingers tangled in her lush golden hair, pushing her all the way down on his erection until it banged the back of her throat.

Holy shit. I'd had threesomes before, but not with a woman like Phee, and certainly not in the great outdoors surrounded by green forest, with a gurgling stream nearby. The fresh air was fucking great on my balls.

I zeroed in on Phee's clit, building up to a suction that threw her over her edge. She ground into my face as she exploded, releasing Jack's dick and screaming loudly enough to scare forest animals for miles.

I gently lifted her up. "Dude, you got any condoms?" I asked Jack.

He reached into the pocket of the jeans he'd thrown on the ground. "Sure do."

"Put one on," I told him, "and give me one."

Phee had sprawled on the ground cloth next to me, wearing a big smile on her face.

"Okay, you," I said, gesturing at her. "Let's get you up and facing that tree. I wanna see you bent over."

Woozy from her orgasm, she stood and stumbled over to the tree, placing her hands on the rough bark. She bent deeply, giving us a view of her wet pussy.

I walked up behind her and reached for her tits. "We're going to take turns fucking you," I said quietly in her ear. "That sound good, baby? You want some more dick?"

"Yeah," she murmured, nodding. She pushed her ass out even further, her curves and folds fucking killing me.

"Jack, after you, my friend," I said, bowing deeply.

Amused, he said, "Why thank you."

He ran his hand up and down Phee's pussy and fisted his cock with his other hand. Positioning himself at her opening, he eased in.

She arched her back, pushing into him to deepen the penetration.

"Oh, yes, Jack, your cock is so good," she cried, her blonde hair flying around her bucking head.

Once fully seated, Jack drove in and out a couple of times, then started pounding our girl's pussy. She screamed and writhed, and just when she was about to come again, he pulled out.

"Wha… where you going?" she whined.

"Patience, baby," Jack said, wiping sweat from his brow. "You're up now, bro." He slapped me on the back.

I positioned myself where my friend had just been and leaned into Phee's ear. "You good, baby? You ready for some more?"

"Mmmm." She shook her head furiously. "Fuck me, Spence. I need it."

"Okay, then." I slowly pushed inside her until I was balls-deep. Reaching around for her clit, I stroked her as I rammed her so full of my hard cock, I had to hold her up.

She screamed as she came, and when she was done, I pulled out for Jack. We switched off like that until we couldn't hold it any longer.

"Phee, turn around now and kneel," I said, and as

she did, Jack and I whipped off our condoms and jacked ourselves until we came on her face and tits.

What a beautiful fucking sight she was to behold, with her mouth open, eagerly accepting our cum like it was gold and rubbing what landed on her tits into her soft skin.

If I could have bottled up that erotic moment, believe me, I sure as hell would have.

CHAPTER 15

PHEE

I think I was learning to like camping.

I zipped my tent closed and lay back in my sleeping bag, surprisingly comfortable thanks to the pad thingy Reggie had loaned me. I was grateful to have my own little crib to escape to and was damn impressed I'd managed to put up a tent by myself. Yeah, it wasn't pretty—it dipped down in the middle because of something I did wrong—but it was otherwise fine. Like I'd let the guys help me, anyway. I didn't want them thinking I was some useless rich girl. They'd already done so much for me, and I wanted to show them I had some level of self-sufficiency. And brains. And grit.

I flicked on my little camping light and pulled out

the paperback I'd sneaked. But I was just too keyed up to read, so I turned the light out and watched the remaining bit of daylight seep through the tent fabric.

Truth was, I couldn't stop thinking about the amazing, earth-shattering threesome I'd just had with Spence and Jack. A *ménage*, I guess it was properly called, which is so weird because that's just French for *household*.

Anyway, I must have come twenty times, and I know they enjoyed the hell out of themselves, too. Afterward, we'd washed up in our little stream and then cooked dinner naked until the bugs came out and Jack got a huge mosquito bite right on his ass. That's when we covered up from head to toe. I would have worn a body condom if I'd had one, that's how much I hated bugs.

But what was cool about being with Spence and Jack was that it wasn't just about getting our rocks off. I was connected to them and could really sense their care. It was amazing. And unexpected.

And Spence's story had rocked me to my core. I was so moved he'd shared it with me. Just goes to show, you never know what someone is going through. To not know where your little girl was... I couldn't even fathom it. And the ex-wife—how could she do something so horrible, to deny her ex his child?

Christ, I thought *I* had problems.

But, I guess you keep moving forward. I mean, where else was there to go?

The campsite we'd snagged was beyond enchanting,

and I was going to hate to leave it to continue hiking toward our next stop. Perhaps I'd be able to talk the guys into giving me a few minutes to do a couple quick sketches. Nothing too fancy.

But on the other hand, now that I was a camping pro, maybe I'd come back here alone.

I heard a little tap on my tent from a falling leaf and turned over to my side, using my sweatshirt as a pillow. I closed my eyes and figured I'd be sleeping with a smile that night.

I heard another leaf fall on my tent and then another and another.

Was it normal for so many leaves to fall at once? I sat up and listened more carefully, until I realized those weren't leaves falling on my tent. They were drops of water.

Rainwater.

I unzipped my tent and stuck my head out. "Guys? Spence? Jack?"

The light flicked on in Jack's tent, and he stuck his head out. "Oh, we're getting some rain."

Spence stuck his head out of his own tent. "It's just a little drizzle. Don't worry, these tents don't leak."

"Oh. Okay." I popped back inside my tent, listening to the rain as I fell asleep.

What was funny was, I had a phone app with the sounds of rain in a forest that I'd *paid* for. And now, here I was, getting the real thing for free. I dozed off feeling pretty damn content.

Until somebody unzipped my tent and woke me with a start, that was.

It was Jack. "Phee, you need to get up." He shined his flashlight into my tent.

What the?

It was *pouring* outside.

"Oh, my god. Can't we just wait in our tents until it stops?" I asked, mildly panicked. The guys had given me what they called *rain gear*, but I hadn't actually planned on using it.

He pulled the hood of his rain jacket tighter when a big drop landed on his face. "Usually, we could. But the stream is rising. Put on your rain gear and boots," he said, gesturing at the pack I'd brought inside my tent with me, "and we'll help you take your tent down."

Well, for fuck's sake. So much for my badass camping experience.

And the stream was rising? What the hell did that mean?

But I pulled the slick nylon rain pants and jacket the guys had given me over my leggings and fleece pullover, and tugged on my socks and boots. I stuffed everything into my backpack and stuck my head out in the pouring rain.

The warm sexiness of our session in the sun the day before was now officially a distant memory.

I stepped out of the tent into a little puddle. Thank god I'd gotten waterproof boots before I'd even set foot on the damn mountain.

The guys were rushing around packing things, so I

pulled out my pack and put the plastic cover on it. I was pretty much ready to go with the exception of my tent, when I noticed the stream.

That quaint little creek bed I'd wiggled my toes in just hours earlier? It was now a rush of muddy brown, and it was only a few feet from our tents.

Jack had not been exaggerating.

"Morning, beautiful," Spence said, pulling the string on my hood tighter after he'd kissed me. "See, if you have the right gear, rain is no trouble at all."

Yeah, right.

"It's not morning. It's still the middle of the night."

"Well, it will be morning soon enough. Give me your tent bag," he said, hand extended.

I reached into my jacket pocket and gave him the small nylon pouch. And, don't you know, he had my tent down and packed in its miniscule bag in about sixty seconds flat.

Cripes.

"Ready?" he asked, attaching it to my backpack.

"I guess. I mean, we're going home now, right?"

The guys looked at each other.

"No. No, we are not," Jack said.

I looked over at Spence.

"We can't get back the way we came because of the water," he said. "Trail's flooded out."

My mind screamed *are you fucking kidding me?* but I kept my mouth shut.

"Lead the way," I grumbled.

The guys seemed to know where we were going

because, in seconds, we were on a new trail. The problem with this one, however, was that it was practically straight *up*.

In the rain.

Which meant it was muddy. And slippery

"Why are we going this way?" I asked. "It's so steep." I blinked rain out of my eyes.

"We have to get to higher ground. The rain's coming down hard enough that there could be flash floods."

"Okay. Stop right there," I said, and they turned to face me. "No one told me our lives could be in danger. You guys checked the weather before we left, right?"

Spence nodded. "Yeah. I mean, it said a small chance of rain. That was all."

I shined my flashlight over at Jack, who rolled his eyes. "Yeah, Spence, it would have been nice if you'd shared that bit of information with us *before* we left."

"C'mon guys," Spence said, continuing up the hill. "Let's get a move on."

"Okay, Spence, we're getting a *move on*, thanks to your not letting us know rain was in the forecast," Jack griped.

"Jack, would you just—"

But I tuned them out after that. They continued to bicker for longer than I cared to listen, first about the rain, then about some grievance one had with the other about a mission years ago, where someone got lost and wasn't found for several days.

Was that going to happen? With all that I'd been

through in recent days, was I going to die in the woods because of a rainstorm? How freaking lame would that be?

I could see the headline:

Heiress, successfully having evaded the assassins that killed her parents,
dies on camping trip.

Thank god for my rain gear. Well, actually, thank Reggie. I was still fairly comfortable with the exception of my wet face and the fact that I was huffing and puffing up a hill. As I reached a switchback that flattened out, I leaned against a tree for a moment to catch my breath and put a little distance between myself and the guys, who were still quarreling.

I took a swig of water after catching my breath and continued. They must have gotten pretty far ahead because I couldn't hear them any longer.

I picked up my pace, figuring I'd either catch up or find them waiting for me. But after about an hour, there was still no sign. And there were no footprints on the path in front of me. Oops.

I'd somehow messed up.

I was fucking lost.

How the hell did that happen? I'd passed a couple forks in the trail, but I'd chosen ones that looked the most traveled. Wasn't that the way the guys were going?

Guess not.

I took several deep breaths, pulled a Clif Bar out of my pocket, and shook the water off my rain jacket. Looking around, I spied a relatively flat spot and made my way over to it. I'd figured I'd wait there until the guys came to find me.

They'd come to find me, right?

Figuring I'd be drier in the tent than out, I decided to re-pitch it so I could hide inside. It was no easy feat in pouring rain, and I was pretty much covered with mud by the time I got it up. But I wanted out of the damn rain. The good news was that I got the sucker up a lot faster this time since I'd watched Spence take it down. I crawled inside of it, dragging all manner of mud and leaves with me, and pulled my pack after me. I'd made a mess of the inside of the tent, but those assholes could clean it when we got home.

If we ever got home.

And when we did, I was going to make some changes. I couldn't hide the rest of my life. I'd leave the country. Maybe go to Mexico first. I could drive there, cover my tracks. Change my name and hang out on the beach. Hire a Spanish tutor to pick up the language faster. I was done waiting around for Morrow or anyone else to decide it was safe for me.

The inside of my tent may have been a mess, but it sure was nice to be out of the rain. I rested my head and dozed until I heard Spence and Jack.

"Hey, she's over here," Spence called.

"Jesus Christ, Phee," Jack said, unzipping my tent and poking his head in.

The rain had let up, thank god, and I was never so happy to see Jack's baby blues.

"Oh, cripes. I fell asleep." But I'd done the right thing in waiting for them to come.

"You gave us a fucking heart attack. Why did you leave the trail?" Jack asked, helping me out of the tent.

"I'm not sure. It wasn't intentional."

Spence started taking down my tent for the second time in a day.

"Well, you were smart to just stay put. It could have been worse if you'd wandered further."

I threw my arms around him and tried hard to swallow the lump in my throat. Our trip had gotten messed up by the rain, and then I'd made it worse by getting separated.

"I'm sorry. I really am."

Spence repacked my tent and smiled. "Don't worry, darling. We'll let you make it up to us."

He smacked my ass as we got back on the trail.

Of course, I smacked his right back.

CHAPTER 16

REGGIE

The cabin was damn quiet with Spence, Jack, and Phee off camping and Axel puttering around the property. I'd taken to sitting on the cabin's front porch with my leg propped up in the hope that my stitches would heal faster. I knew my effort was probably futile because the ER doc had told me I needed a full two weeks, maybe even longer, since the drill had, well, drilled the shit out of my thigh.

God was I pissed at myself over the stupid accident. My leg hurt like hell, and I couldn't walk far because I was limping like an old man. At least aspirin helped with the pain. To say I was getting cabin fever was an understatement.

One of the upsides of being semi-laid up was

having time to reflect. Sounds totally cheeseball, I know, but that shit happens when you're not busy enough.

Despite some initial reservations, I was really digging our houseguest, Phee. I mean, she was a little clueless when it came to real life—I guess as a result of having been brought up rich and pampered—but she had no illusions about who she was, and I respected that. Nothing was worse than a beautiful woman who acted like her shit didn't stink.

What a different life I'd had from hers. I'd grown up dirt-poor, so poor that the day after high school graduation, I'd run to the nearest Army recruiting office. It was the only ticket out of my rotten life, and I was prepared to work hard to make sure I didn't end up back there. In fact, I would have gone the *day* of graduation, but I was busy getting drunk with my buddies.

It was the last time I'd ever see most of them. Five died in a drunk-driving accident late that night. The only reason I hadn't been with them was that I had to get up at seven a.m. and didn't want to fuck up my recruiting appointment. I was off to basic before they'd even had the funerals.

Last I'd ever see of that town, too. Talk about leaving shit behind.

I'd left behind my mom, too, although that wasn't saying much. She'd chased off my dad before I was one, and she'd always made it pretty clear she didn't really want me around, either. I sent her a Christmas card most years, and I'd put a little cash in it if I could. Guess there are some people we just never give up on.

And when she got wind I was making real money—not enlisted soldier money, but private sector security money—boy, did she sing a different tune. It was like I was her new best friend. She'd gotten pretty old, so I couldn't really deny her.

So, yeah, I was a little gun-shy about who I spent time with. And even though I might look like a tough guy with my tattoos and tribal jewelry, I was still, basically, a softhearted motherfucker.

Not that I would ever tell anyone that.

Phee had been more on my mind than I wanted to admit, and not just because I loaned her my best camping gear—the best shit money could buy.

So, I was freaked when she, Spence, and Jack came out of the woods while I was sitting there on the porch trying to read my military history book. The three were a couple of days overdue because of the rain we'd been getting, but I'd gotten the heads-up when they notified us via walkie-talkie. What got me was that I didn't think I'd ever seen a more bedraggled woman in my life. And to think it was Phee's first camping trip.

I pushed myself out of my rocking chair and limped down the porch steps to meet my sorry crew and grab Phee's pack off her back.

"Jesus, guys. You look like you've been through the ringer," I said. "You okay, Phee?"

I'd seen the guys dirty and disheveled before. After all, we'd done enough missions together where you had to go a week or longer without bathing or even changing your socks. But to see Phee, her face and arms covered with grime and mosquito bites, and her hair hanging around her face in dirty strings, just about knocked me over.

"Give me your pack, Phee," I said, taking it off her shoulders.

"Thanks, Reggie," she said cheerfully, and in spite of her condition. "How's the leg?"

"Sore. I have the stitches in for a while longer, but the pain has subsided. So, how was the trip?"

They looked at Phee.

"There were some challenges with the rain, but it was actually pretty fun," she said, smiling.

Damn. I always said you couldn't keep a good woman down.

"All right," I said, looking them over. "Don't wear those shoes in the house." I pointed at their muddy boots.

"Yes, *Mom*," Spence said, untying his laces and peeling off his soggy socks.

Phee grabbed a seat in one of the front porch rocking chairs and leaned back with closed eyes. "Oh, my god, Reggie, we had a good time, but it is *so* good to be back. Did Axel take good care of you?" She sighed and propped her bare feet—the only part of her that was clean, probably because they were covered the whole time—up on the porch railing.

"He did the bare minimum. About what I expected," I said with a laugh.

With an abundance of enthusiasm, she shared with me the details of her trip, how she got lost, how they had to detour around a flash flood, and how, when they ran out of food, Jack caught a couple fish.

I had a feeling she was leaving out the hanky-panky I was *sure* took place, but that was fine. I wasn't the kiss-and-tell type, either.

"Geez, Phee, sounds like you're ready for your own survival TV show. I can see it now—*Survivorbabe*."

She threw her head back and burst out laughing, the little tits under her dirty T-shirt shaking just so.

Christ, I was a perv. Poor thing had just been through the ringer and I was feeling her up with my eyes.

"It's good to have you back, sweetie," I said as soon as the other guys had gone into the house.

It wasn't that I had anything to hide, but rather, I just didn't want Spence or Jack, or anybody for that manner, to hear me being a softie.

And my risk paid off. She reached for my hand and smiled at me, those damn big eyes doing a job on me and my dick.

I stood in front of her and extended my hands. "Let's get you showered and into some clean clothes."

She jumped up, putting her face close to mine. Really close.

"I think I can handle this on my own."

Was she flirting? Or blowing me off?

"Well, I'm not sure. I mean, I think you've had quite the adventure and now deserve a little pampering. The kind of pampering only a guy like me can provide."

She looked at me with a crooked smile. "Well, then. Let's go," she said, leading me by the hand into the house, her short shorts showing off the cheeks of her ass quite nicely.

Damn Spence and Jack. They'd gotten to admire this view for days while I sat home with a bad leg, jerking off to porn and suffering through Axel's cooking.

But I had my fingers crossed that might be changing, and hopefully, that very night.

"I gotta tell you, Phee, even filthy dirty, you're still pretty goddamn hot."

She nudged me in the ribs as we walked, laughing. "Yeah, right. I'm feeling really sexy about now." She looked down at her fingernails, where the red paint had come off in large chips and the edges were snagged and broken.

"I'm a disgusting mess."

"Well, just to make sure you come out super clean, I think I'll join you in the shower," I said, my cock getting hard just thinking about it.

She stopped at her bedroom door. "You do? Well, I think it could be pretty tight in there. You sure there's room?" she asked, cocking her head and leaving me dying to rip off her clothes and take her right there in the hallway, dirt and other objections be damned.

I bent to press my lips to hers, and her hands found their way to my face.

"Okay. Get in here," I said, pulling her to the bathroom.

"On a serious note, Reg, what about your leg?" she asked.

I looked down at the bandage on my leg. "I can get the stitches wet now. It's been long enough."

I peeled off her clothes and then mine and led her to the warm shower where I started with her hair. I rinsed it until the water ran clear of dirt and then lathered it up for a nice scalp massage.

"Oh, my god, where did you learn to do that?" she murmured.

I pressed my cock against her round ass, where it slid around nicely thanks to the stream of water.

"I'll never reveal the source of my many talents. Sorry, darling."

She spun to face me, holding the soap. Her hands were full of foamy lather.

"Whatcha gonna do with that, dirty girl?" I asked, pulling on her taut nipples.

Her eyes flickered, and her voice dropped to a husky level I'd not heard before. "I'm gonna soap up your cock. Gonna get it nice and clean. I can see how hard you already are. And then, I'm gonna slide it up my ass."

Holy. Fucking. Shit.

Where did this woman come from?

"Didn't know you were so naughty, bad girl. But I'll fuck you in the ass like you've never had it."

She shivered in the hot shower, and goose bumps exploded across her skin.

Yeah. I had her right where I wanted her.

The little vixen soaped up my cock so good, I had to fight off exploding right then in her hands.

"Turn around," I growled.

I lubed my finger with soap and explored her tight hole. With my other hand, I reached around to massage her clit and kept my lips on her neck under the spray of shower water.

"Mmmm," she moaned.

"You sure you want it this way?" I asked, notching myself at her behind.

She nodded and reached back to her ass cheeks. "Yeah, Reggie. I do want you in my ass. Please," she whispered.

I eased in just a bit to give her time to adjust, and just as I was about to enter her further, she pushed back on me until I was buried balls-deep.

Did wonders never cease?

"Fuck!" I groaned as her tight walls squeezed me nearly to the point of discomfort.

I eased out, and she pushed right back on me. Who knew our little rich girl loved having her ass full of cock?

"God, Reggie, it's so good," she moaned in between gasps.

She reached between her legs to feel me sliding in and out. Seconds later, she exploded into an orgasm that left her legs trembling so badly, I had to hold her up like a limp doll.

I pulled out just in time to spurt on her pretty ass cheek, with her holding the shower wall to steady her shuddering.

I finished washing her, then helped her out of the shower and dried her with thick white towels. I walked her to bed, where I helped her crawl under her fluffy down comforter, and I crawled in right behind her. By the time I turned out the light and wrapped my arms around her, she was already snoozing.

The woman was so hot even her cute girl-snore was sexy.

CHAPTER 17

PHEE

Cripes was it nice to be back in a real bed with soft sheets and pillows, in a warm, dry, clean bedroom. I didn't care how simple my room was—it was a castle compared to a muddy, wet tent.

I wasn't kidding when I said I'd enjoyed camping. I really had. But I suspect one of the best things about it was coming home and realizing how good you had it. I mean, why would anyone go, otherwise? Schlepping your stuff, pitching tents, building fires, and peeing outdoors were not the most comfortable of things.

Guess you had to look at the payoff—fresh air, exercise, and if you were as lucky as me, multiple zesty sessions with two of the hottest men on the planet.

Seriously, Jack and Spence were the kind of men

who are created only once—deliciously muscular, fit, and strong, but also so fucking handsome they looked like they walked out of a Ralph Lauren magazine.

My professor and my football player. What more could a girl ask for?

And yet, I did. The moment I got home, I was seduced by Reggie's attentions. Reggie, my almost silver fox, with his salt-and-pepper temples and craggy tanned face. He'd indulged my wildest need when he'd taken a shower with me, in addition to cleaning me and putting me to bed.

A girl could get used to this stuff.

Then why was I thinking of getting the hell out of there?

The last thing I remembered from the night before was Reggie tucking me in while I was still nice and warm from our shower. Next I knew, sun was streaming into my bedroom, I was alone, and the house was dead quiet.

Yeah, these guys were special, no doubt about it. It was no wonder Morrow wanted me to stay with them while he tracked down my parents' killers. But they weren't mine, and neither was this mountaintop home. I had to make my own life and stop being a bother to the guys.

That's why I'd swiped a set of keys from the basket near the door when I'd come home from camping. They were just sitting there, almost calling to me, and I reached for them without thinking. They represented, for a moment, the new life I wanted to build.

I shoved as much as I could into a duffel, figuring I'd send someone to get the rest of my stuff somewhere down the road, when I was settled and safe. Or maybe not. All that crap that was sitting in the corner of my room? I'd not touched it since I'd arrived, nor had I missed any of it.

It was just stuff. Pain-in-the-ass stuff. Things I'd once thought I'd needed and dragged everywhere with me. But I'd learned a few things in recent days. That nothing was more important than my parents, whom I would never have the opportunity to thank for all they'd done for me, and that all I really needed was my sketchpad, pencils, paints, and a couple good books to read. And my moisturizer. The rest was gravy. Or an albatross, depending on how you looked at it.

But yeah, I was done with Savage Mountain. I'd miss the guys, but my current wantonness couldn't continue indefinitely. I mean, it wasn't like anything would come of my messing around with them, right? My plan was to drive straight through to Mexico with as few stops as possible, letting only Morrow know where I was. He could inform the guys, if he wanted. It wasn't like I'd ever see them again.

Although, that thought made my heart hurt a bit.

I quietly opened my bedroom door and crept toward the kitchen, guessing no one was around but not wanting to risk getting caught with my bag. When I looked outside, I found one of the trucks gone and a note tacked to the front door: *gone to town. see you later this afternoon.*

If memory served, I knew the way to town. So, I knew to go in the opposite direction, at least initially, to avoid the guys. I grabbed some fruit from the kitchen and ran to the closest truck, which happened to belong to the keys I'd swiped.

I stood outside the truck, bag over my shoulder, momentarily frozen and unable to open the door and just get in. So much about what I was looking at meant freedom—freedom to start my own, new life. But it also meant leaving the place that had saved me after my parents died. The guys had been stern, sure, but also loving. And kind. And attentive.

But the keys found their way into the car door and then the ignition, and next thing I knew, I was speeding down the mountain, eager to reach the turnoff for town. An hour past it, I finally began to relax. I was conflicted as hell, forcing myself to keep moving forward without thinking too hard before I changed my mind about everything and turned back.

I felt naked without my cell phone. I'd left that behind because I knew those special ops guys would find me in a New York minute if I had it on me. First chance I got, I'd pick up a burner phone in case of emergency. I also had to let Morrow know I'd hit the road. He wouldn't be happy about it, but I couldn't let him run my life, even if he was one of my father's most trusted advisors.

After several hours' drive, when I could barely keep my eyes open, I pulled into a small motel in the middle of nowhere. The sleepy clerk gave me a key, and I parked the truck in back, out of view of the highway.

"India?" I said as soon as she answered the call I made from my motel room. By calling her I'd know whether the guys were on my trail.

"*Where are you?*" she demanded. "One of your guys called me. Said he got my number out of your phone and that you'd taken off with one of their trucks."

How did they do that? Actually, I didn't want to know. Those guys could do some crazy shit.

"I decided to leave. I have to live my life, India. I'm going to Mexico."

I could hear her pacing. "Okay. Where you at? I'll come get you."

I pulled the drapes shut on my motel room after peering out the window. I'd never stayed in a motel, and it reminded me of *Psycho.*

I thought quickly. I needed to put her off.

"I don't know, India. I've got to do this on my own. When I get settled in, I'll let you know where I am."

She sighed impatiently. "Well, I really think it would be better if you weren't alone, but okay. Where in Mexico are you going?"

I shrugged. "Don't know yet."

I could practically hear her rolling her eyes, that's how well I knew her. "You've *got* to have some idea. I mean, Mexico is a huge country."

"Why are you being so pushy?" I snapped. "I told you I'd let you know."

She was silent for a moment. "Oh. I get it. Fine."

I looked out the window again. I was starving but not sure where to find food at that hour, much less if I should even risk leaving. I pulled out one of the Clif Bars I'd swiped from the cabin and took a small nibble.

"Hey, Phee, before you leave, do you think I could ask for a small loan?"

'A small loan' for India actually meant 'will you give me some money that I probably will never pay back?'

And for the first time ever, a wave of irritation swept over me that she was asking for money. *Again.*

She might have been my best friend, but I was never entirely sure how she got by. She didn't come from a family like mine, and she didn't work consistently. I'd always figured she'd inherited some cash somewhere along the line, but that it wasn't quite enough to sustain her lifestyle or enable her to keep up with our group of friends. I'd offered her money once when she couldn't afford to join everyone on an expensive trip, and I'd been supplementing her ever since.

I'd not minded, not at all. God knew I had pretty much unlimited resources, and she'd been a good friend to me.

But something about her request this time rubbed me the wrong way. It felt… insensitive, somehow. Like, really selfish, considering I was essentially running for my life.

"Um no, India. I don't think I can help you. I'm not even sure how I'll get money for myself." I'd not spent much of the wad of cash Morrow had given me, but I needed to make it last.

Her voice got shrill. "What do you mean? You have tons of money. I only need a little."

Really?

My suspicion that this woman might not be much of a friend was quickly being proven correct.

"India, I need to go now. I'll get back in touch when I can."

"Wait, Phee—"

But I didn't hear any more. I'd hung up the room phone and sat on the bed, fighting back the despair that had become a frequent visitor of mine. Actually, more like a permanent resident.

Fuck, fuck, fuck.

Parents? Dead and gone. Boyfriend? A murderous traitor. BFF? A major sponge.

So, I let it out, the grief, hurt, despair, and anger. At first, my shoulders heaved, and then, the dam broke, my body racked with sobs so loud, I had to turn on the TV. I fell to the floor and clawed at the carpet on my hands and knees, as if hurting something inanimate would transfer a little of my pain.

I must have spent at least an hour on the floor, weak from my battering emotions, but also strangely relieved that I'd somehow lived through them.

I knew they'd eventually be back, this maelstrom of feeling, and possibly with a vengeance, but when they did return, I'd face them again. What choice did I have?

I was going to fucking make it. One way or the other.

My next call was to Morrow. I had no idea where in

the world he was, given that he was a big security guru, but I was pretty sure, even if it was the middle of the night for him, he'd pick up.

"Hello?" he answered, attempting to disguise the sleep in his voice.

I guess with a profession like his, you never got a good night's sleep.

"Morrow," I said simply.

Bedclothes rustled in the background. "Phee? Jesus, where are you? Are you okay? The guys from Savage let me know you were gone."

"I'm fine, Morrow, just fine. I left on my own. No one knows where I am."

"At the moment, no one knows, but the people who killed your parents and who are now after you are very adept at finding the people they are looking for. You cannot be out there on your own, Phee. You cannot successfully run from them on your own."

The urgency in his voice sent shivers down my spine. I mean, of course I knew there were bad guys after me, but it hadn't really sunk in how persistent they would be. Could I really move someplace like Mexico, live under the radar, where they'd still find me?

"Well, Morrow, I think I can keep a low profile. I'm going to Mexico. No one will find me there."

"No, Phee. That will not work—"

Impatience shot up my spine. "Then I want you to get me to Mexico. Set up someplace safe for me, where I can live anonymously, that only you know about. I want my own home, not some place where I'm just crashing."

He sighed deeply after a moment. "Okay. I'll help you. I'll get you out of the country and into a new life, if that's what you really want."

Oh, thank god.

"I knew you'd help, Morrow."

"But there's one thing, Phee. Setting this up will take some time and planning. For the time being, I need you to go back up to Savage Mountain."

"Morrow—"

"It's non-negotiable, Phee. Either you go back now, or I will not help you. I cannot protect you when you are out on your own like you are right now. Your father would never forgive me if I let anything happen."

At the mention of my father, something clicked.

Dad. I missed him so much. Mom, too.

If he were here, he'd talk me out of just taking off. It was like Morrow was channeling him.

"All right. I'll go back. But Morrow, please keep in mind that I'm ready to start my own life in my own home."

"I got it, Phee. I'm going to call the guys to get you so you don't have to drive back alone. Just promise me you'll stay right where you are."

"Yeah. Just promise me I'll have a life again."

CHAPTER 18

JACK

She did it again. She fucking took off.

I'd thought we had a great time camping, the crappy weather and flash floods notwithstanding. She was a trooper, and she never complained. I didn't know many women who could pull that off, much less one who came from Phee's background.

Other people might have thought she was just spoiled, but I'd seen her handle some tough shit in the days she'd been with us on the mountain. I don't know that I'd hold things together if I'd been through all she had.

The woman was finding strength in places she didn't know she had any.

When we first got back from our trip to town and

found her missing, we thought we'd done something to drive her away. But after we examined our behavior, we couldn't put our finger on a single thing. I mean, we got along great with her, and, in fact, I think we were all pretty damn attached to her.

She was gorgeous and fucking sexy as hell, smart, interesting, and artistic.

Talking with Morrow, both before and after she'd let us know where she was, left us even more confused. Taking off on her own, again? Why?

Did she think we were after her money? She'd mentioned more than once having 'friends' who hit her up for cash, and I knew she was wary of users. But we guys had our own dough. The work of private security contracting was very lucrative. It's what had made her father so successful, after all.

So, when Morrow called us to go get her and told us he'd talked sense into her, he'd simply said she was ready to start a new life. Didn't have anything to do with us guys.

Not that that made it easier. We didn't talk about it, but I couldn't deny I was a little pissed she'd bailed without a word.

So, we drove down to get her, mostly in silence and lost in thought, I'm guessing each of us wondering why she'd take off with her life in danger as it was.

Seriously, did she not realize what she was up against? Or was she just in denial?

The ride back, once we'd picked her up from the shitty motel she'd checked into, was just as quiet. She rode with Axel and me while Spence and Reggie drove the truck she'd 'borrowed' from us.

"Phee. You're pretty quiet. You okay?" I asked. I was glad I'd grabbed the back seat next to her so I could make sure she was all right.

Looking out the window, she nodded slowly. "I feel badly. I shouldn't have put you guys through this. It was selfish of me. I thought, for a moment that I could just drive away into the sunset and it would make no difference to anyone. But it's not that simple."

She looked at me with a small smile, one that seemed like it might be asking for forgiveness.

"Morrow said you were ready to strike out on your own?" Axel asked. "I don't understand why you felt you had to leave. Or how you thought it might be an improvement over your current situation."

She shrugged. "Yeah. I thought I might be able to make that work."

"Well, if there's anything we can do to make you more comfortable, just let us know. I mean, we don't want you to feel like you're dying to get the hell away from us. You're welcome to stay as long as Morrow feels you're safer with us, but you can also stay beyond that. I think I can speak for all of us when I say, we like having you around."

Her bottom lip trembled and a small tear rolled down her cheek.

"No. No, it's not that at all. I love the cabin, and you guys have been nothing but good to me. I guess, I was starting to feel like a burden." She sniffled hard.

I reached for her hand. "You are not a bother. I mean, look at you. Smart, interesting, gorgeous. There's not a chance in hell we'd ever want you to leave."

I pulled her to me, and she looked up at me from under wet eyelashes, a real smile spreading across her face.

"Guess I just lost my mind for a moment." She closed her eyes and took a big inhale. "I thought I'd drive all the way to Mexico. How stupid was that?"

Axel nodded. "That's a long damn drive, no doubt about it."

"What I'd really wanted to do, before my parents—" she hesitated for a moment, "—before they died, was to study art at the Sorbonne. That had been my dream."

"Paris isn't going anywhere. You'll get there. You know you will."

She nodded hopefully, her face brightening. "Thank you, Jack. I actually owe you all a big thanks. I'll never be able to repay what you've done for me."

I leaned closer and rubbed my nose in her hair.

She tilted her head and leaned toward me, pressing her lips so softly to mine, I barely felt anything beyond the warmth of her breath.

"How's that for repayment?" she asked, pulling back with a wicked smile.

Axel looked at us from the front seat. "Cripes, guys, get a room."

"I had a room. We just left it behind," Phee said.

"And what a room it was. Had you ever been in a motel?" Axel asked.

She knew she was being teased and was a good sport about it. "Oh, yeah. They're my preferred type of travel accommodation. In fact, I have stayed in them so much, I have points and often get free nights, if you ever want to go back."

"We may take you up on that," Axel said.

Phee leaned forward. "Axe, why don't you pull over at that scenic outlook up ahead?"

He took a quick glance at me in the rearview mirror and made a turn with the wheel. We pulled into the small rocky parking lot overlooking a beautiful valley.

The best news was that no one else was there.

Axel got out and opened Phee's door, taking her by the arm. "I have a request of you, Phee."

"Yeah?"

He put his hands on his hips and looked more serious than I'd ever seen him. "You have to promise not to take off again. You don't know what that puts us through, especially Morrow. The man is on the other side of the world worried about you, when he thought you were in good hands with us."

Phee looked at him with wide eyes.

"I need your word," he said. "We can't lock you in your room twenty-four seven."

"Yes, Axel. Yes, I promise. I'm not going anywhere," she said.

He threw me a glance, and I nodded back.

"C'mere, baby," I said. I opened the back door and

bent her forward over the seat. I pulled her jeans down and slipped my fingers into her soaking wet folds.

"Mmmm, Jack. That's nice," she said, wiggling her ass in the air.

Axel crawled in the other side of the car, knelt in front of her, and ran his hands through her lush hair. She looked up, reached for his fly, and whipped out his raging erection. From where I stood behind her, I saw it disappear into her mouth, and a big smile spread across Axel's face.

With her pretty ass in the air, I stepped her feet apart and crouched to reach her with my tongue. I lapped her from front to back, leaving her shivering with delight. Axel rocked his hips to give her more, and she responded by sucking him harder. I ripped off my shirt and opened my jeans, rolling on a condom from my pocket, and positioned myself between her pussy lips. Leaning forward, I put my hands on her tits and inched inside her.

"You good, baby?" I asked in her ear.

Her mouth full of Axel, she nodded and pushed back against my cock until I was balls-deep inside her. I pistoned slowly at first, the sunshine brushing my bare skin just like it had when we were camping. My balls pulled in tight as I pounded. But I held off. I wanted her to come first.

My naughty girl reached back and pulled herself open so I could drive even deeper. That's when Axel groaned loudly, dropping his head back and thrusting his hips forward one last time. Phee swallowed everything he gave her, and I thrust one more time. Trembling overtook her as an orgasm hit like a tidal wave. She screamed as I pumped her, coming over and over, until I finally unloaded in her tight hole.

Axel and I got into the back seat and pulled her to us. Plain and simple, she was wiped out, her head hanging limp while her body rippled with mini-convulsions. She burrowed her head against my neck with eyes closed, holding one of each of our hands.

"Phee?" I said.

"Mmmm?" She looked up at me.

"With, um, entertainment like this, I would think you'd be pretty happy with us guys."

She raised her head and looked at both of us. "I am happy with you guys. I guess I split because I wasn't so sure how happy you were with me."

Axel laughed. "Well, I think now you know."

CHAPTER 19

PHEE

Cripes, was I an asshole. I mean, the guys in the cabin had really bent over backward to make me feel welcome, and what did I do?

Split in one of their vehicles, was unreachable by cell, and left them wondering what the fuck was up.

Not exactly the actions of a grateful guest.

The guys were awesome. Beyond awesome, actually. And if I were completely honest with myself, I'd admit I was falling for them.

All of them.

How messed up was that? I couldn't fall for four guys. Actually, I couldn't fall for any of them. My eventual plan was to move to Paris, and that was far from Savage Mountain. Too far.

But they were all so goddamn gorgeous, like high-end racecars tuned to perfection, each different enough from the other that it was impossible to say which was best.

I wanted them all. Desperately.

Which was why I had to get out of there as soon as I could. I didn't want to risk falling for any of them, much less all four, and risk tearing apart their lives. The mountain was just a way station for me, someplace to hang during a difficult transition. Morrow would let me know when the coast was clear and I could continue living my life, hopefully much as I had before, without looking over my shoulder every minute of every day.

And how could I be with anyone in the private security business? It had already taken my parents from me. I couldn't bear losing anyone else the same way. It would kill me. I knew it would.

So yeah, I'd pretty much been a fool to leave like I had. It could have seriously fucked up—or ended—my life, not to mention made a lot of trouble for the guys in the cabin.

I just needed to keep my head down, work on my paintings, read my books, and keep my heart to myself.

There was a knock on my open bedroom door, and Axel poked his head in.

"Hey, sweetie, you getting all settled back in?" he asked.

I looked up at him, taken as I always was by his tough-boy ear plugs and spiky hair, and of course, our naughty little session on the way back from the motel.

"Hey, Axel. Yeah. I'm good." I sat on the edge of my bed and looked at all my crap in the corner. Evening dresses. High heels. What had I been thinking?

He came in and took a seat next to me.

"You don't look too happy. I know you were trying to leave town. Sorry you're still stuck here."

The compassion in his eyes made me so ashamed I'd taken their hospitality—and care—for granted.

"Axel, I *so* don't deserve you guys."

He burst out laughing. "What?"

"To make you think the reason I left was that I didn't want to be around you guys? You're the only thing in my life that has gone right."

He put an arm around me and kissed me on the head. "Okay. So, anything particular getting you down at the moment? Or just the general situation?"

I thought hard.

"You know, I had an uncomfortable conversation with my best friend over the phone when I was at the hotel."

I filled him in on how India had, one, wanted money, and two, was very insistent I tell her where I was.

I looked up from my wringing hands and found Axel wearing an expression I'd not seen before. The best way I could describe it was a mixture of suspicion and anger.

He took a deep breath. "Phee, I don't like the sound

of this, and I think your instincts are right on. There's something fishy about that conversation. I'm glad you told me."

"Really? Why?"

"One, I think the asking for money thing is just rude, especially considering where your life is at the moment. But second, why would she need to know so badly where you were? It's not like she was going to fly out and pick you up, especially if she's broke."

"Wh… why do you think she wanted to know, then?" I asked.

He rolled his shoulders as if to relieve stress. "I have a bad feeling about India, your friend. Something doesn't feel right, and I usually trust my gut. All us guys do. It's part of our training."

"She's my best friend. Do you think she's up to something?"

He stood, pacing the room. "She introduced you to Sammy, right?

"Yeah, but I don't think—

"I want to look into this. See if there's something more than meets the eye."

"How? What will you do?"

He stopped pacing. "We'll… create a scenario. You'll be the decoy."

What the hell did that mean? I wanted to find out if my best friend was up to something, but that didn't mean I wanted to be a sitting duck.

"I'll tell you what," he said. "Let's meet up with your friend and figure out what's going on."

"Really? I don't know, Axe. I mean, there's probably nothing going on. She was just pushing for my location because she cares about me."

"Like your friend Sammy?"

That one hit me in the pit of my stomach.

He pulled me into a hug. "I don't mean to upset you. But the world your father operated in is not one for the faint of heart. He protected you from that, but since he's not around anymore, you need to learn to protect yourself."

When he put it like that, all the despair in the world welled up in me and my heart broke all over again. But this time it wasn't sadness.

No, I was pissed. I was going to find out who killed my parents and make them pay.

I was going to learn from Axel and the other guys how my dad's world worked so I could find a way to survive in the situation he left for me.

"When do we start?" I asked.

CHAPTER 20

AXEL

"Do you really think India can lead us to my parents' murderers, Axel?" Phee asked as we drove our rental car away from the airport. We'd traveled overnight and were exhausted. But that didn't mean Phee wasn't ready to help put my plan in motion. I'd seen the look in her eyes before. It was hunger for revenge. The woman was angry, and she had a right to be.

The other guys in the house were going to follow us by one day. We all cared about her, that much was clear. But who knew yet how long she'd stay with us. I had to admit that if she did split, I sure as hell would miss her. Never thought I'd say that about another woman after my wife took off, but there I was. Smitten by the last person in the world I thought I'd find myself falling for.

Shit. Did I say *falling for*?

Goddamn.

My initial impressions about Phee were proven wrong. Completely wrong. I mean, yeah, she came from a rich family and was sheltered, but that didn't mean she wasn't a strong woman. She had character in spades and could give as good as she got.

And she was stunning and sexy as hell on top of it all.

Who knew a woman like that even existed? I wouldn't have believed it if she'd not just walked into our lives on Savage Mountain and, without even trying, pretty much turned everything upside down. The energy she brought to the house was a breath of fresh air.

So, I tried not to think about the possibility of her leaving. I mean, I guess it was inevitable. She wanted a life. She wanted more than Savage Mountain could offer. Sure, our place was an amazing little slice of Heaven, but it wasn't Paris. It wasn't the Sorbonne.

It wasn't home. Not to her, anyway.

"Okay, I'm placing my call to India," Phee said, grabbing her phone. "Are we ready?"

I veered into morning rush-hour traffic on the way to our hotel.

"Yeah. Are you clear on what to say?"

Phee took a deep breath. "I think so. Get her to the house, right? Tell her I'm back at my parents'?"

I chanced a look at Phee and found she was not only tired, but also nervous. Hell, I would be too if I were about to test a friend to see what they were really about. And I hoped to god my intuition was wrong. I didn't want Phee to be down one best friend after she'd just lost her parents and the guy she was dating.

"Exactly. Let's aim to meet her later today."

She reached for my hand over the rental car console. "Hey, Axe, did you happen to tell Morrow what we were up to?"

Shit. I knew that question was coming.

"I did not. Probably should have, but I didn't."

Probably should have. That was an understatement. Morrow was going to lose his shit when he found out I took Phee on a mission. But I didn't care. The time was ripe to see if India was up to anything. If she wasn't, great. But if she was, then we'd not missed our window of opportunity.

Phee tapped her phone screen while we pulled into the hotel parking lot. "Hey, India? It's me."

I heard India's strident voice in the background.

Phee nodded. "Yes, yes, I'm fine. Hey, guess what? I'm back in town."

More squawking from the phone at Phee's ear.

"Yeah, can you believe it? I figured it was time to come home for a while." She glanced at me, and I gave her a wink and a thumbs-up.

"I want to see you, too. Tell ya what. Let's meet at my parents' at—" she paused, "—five-ish this evening.

We can drink some of their good wine and then maybe catch dinner."

She looked at me, her eyes full of fear. "No, India, I don't know if the staff will be there. I would guess that Morrow kept them on, but whether or not they'll be there, I don't know. Why? Does it matter?"

Phee rubbed her hand over her face, clearly accepting that something was out of the ordinary. My heart ached for the woman. We didn't know anything definitive yet, but to even *think* your best friend might be betraying you?

Devastating.

She swiped her phone closed, her eyes full of tears.

"Why would she do that?" she asked quietly.

I reached across the car and put my arm around her. "We don't know anything yet. But I will say, if someone got to her and offered her the right amount of money, she might value that above all. Some people are like that. And we're about to find out."

We grabbed our bags and headed into the hotel lobby to register with one of my fake IDs left from my time as a special operative. I didn't use them much these days, but all us guys kept them because they came in handy when we did.

We settled into our room and ordered some food. We both desperately needed a nap before the evening activities ahead, and I wanted to make sure we were well rested.

But we had to take care of business first. Before Phee dozed off, we went over our plan one more time.

CHAPTER 21

PHEE

Holy shit, I was setting up my own best friend. How whacked was that?

Axel had said it was necessary to find out what she was up to, given the behavior he'd found suspicious. But all I could think about was all the good times we'd had together, hanging out, partying, traveling, and bellyaching over silly injustices the world had thrown our way.

Little did I know what real hardship was. I had to lose my parents to understand.

And now we were on our way to their house, which they left one morning, to fly to a meeting, never to return home.

I didn't know how it would be, seeing their house, which I hadn't been to since Morrow had spirited me off to Savage Mountain. I'd gone there as soon as I'd gotten the devastating news—I don't know why—maybe to try and feel their presence? But Morrow had told me to get out right away. I'd returned to my apartment to pack, just as he'd told me, and then a driver came—the one who'd left me at the side of the road to wait for the guys.

My parents' massive house came into view, and tears sprang to my eyes when I saw the overgrown front yard and dead flowers in the garden. My mother would have had a fit if she'd known the house was looking such a mess. I guessed Morrow had told the housekeeper and gardener to stay away, but why? Surely, the house still required upkeep.

Perhaps for their own safety?

I remembered the last time I'd been there. In the minutes after I'd found out about my parents' deaths, I'd wandered aimlessly around their house and ended up in their bedroom, where I stared at my dad's slippers and my mom's perfume bottles. I wanted to touch them, but for some reason, I couldn't. I was frozen with shock. So, I hadn't had the chance to grab anything of theirs before Morrow told me to leave for my own safety.

Would I have the chance to, now? I just wanted something small. I wanted to feel them with me.

Speaking of safety, I was borderline terrified—one,

that we were walking into a dangerous situation, and two, that I might find out something about my best friend that would break my heart.

Please, India, don't hurt me.

I pulled the baseball cap Axel had gotten me lower over my eyes, ensuring my long hair was tucked up inside it securely. He'd also gotten me some cheap gas station sunglasses and warned me not to take them off. It wasn't the world's best disguise, but it would at least ensure that at a quick glance, it wasn't obviously me.

To be extra careful, however, Axel had me get in the back seat. I sank down as low as I could and pointed out my parents' house.

"Okay," he said, checking it out. "I'm gonna drive by a time or two to see if anyone else is watching it like we are."

I craned my neck to peek, then sank back down. "How will you know if anyone's watching?"

He winked at me in the rearview mirror. "The government spent a lot of time and money training guys like me. I can visually sweep an area in a matter of seconds and have a pretty good sense of what's going on."

I watched two cars pull up to my parents' house. "Who is that?"

"Good question."

He parked the car far enough down the street that we wouldn't be seen and began to watch it with tiny binoculars.

"What can you see? Tell me."

"Two cars with two guys apiece. One from each car just got out and are walking up to the front door."

I swallowed a big gulp from the water bottle I'd brought to try and stave off the nausea churning in my stomach.

India was betraying me. She'd crossed to the other side and was selling me out. I didn't think I could have been more heartbroken had she tried to do me in me herself.

But my devastation quickly transitioned to anger. I'd been a good friend to her, just like she'd been to me. I'd supported all her crazy ups and downs and had financed the bulk of our activities, not because I *had* to but because I wanted to. And she was selling me out?

To assassins?

Did she have something to do with my parents' deaths?

"I'm gonna kill her," I mumbled.

"Hey, hey, easy there," Axel said. "You're not killing anyone. That's not your job."

My fists were balled so tight, my fingers were white.

"It might not be my job. But it's my right. If I find out she had anything to do with my parents—"

Axel grabbed for his ringing cell phone. "Hey, Spence? Yeah, I'll send you my coordinates. Stand by."

He tapped something into his phone and turned from the front seat to face me.

"The other guys are on their way. They'll be here in minutes."

Axel started the car and inched it closer to the house.

"Where did the guys go who got out of the cars?" I asked.

"Probably inside the house," he said, pulling up a few more feet.

"How'd they get into my parents' house?" I cried.

He turned to look at me over the back seat again. "Phee. Are you really asking that?"

Oh.

Who were these fucking people who inhabited the dark corners of society, who could get any information they wanted, find anyone they were looking for, and get inside places they shouldn't be?

Just then, India pulled into the driveway like she had a hundred times before. She walked up to the front door in her usual short skirt and sky-high platforms like she always wore. Just when she pressed the doorbell, Jack, Spence, and Reggie screeched up and jumped out of their car.

"Time to move," Axel said, racing the car down the street and hopping out to train his gun on the guys in the getaway cars.

Jack raced up to the house and got a grip on a terrified India, and Spence entered the house. I heard gunshots and leaned out the car to get sick.

Was somebody shot? What if it was one of my guys? All because of me.

I pushed myself out the car door in spite of the fact that Reggie was yelling at me to stay, but the moment the guys in the getaway car spotted me, they raised their guns toward me. I froze, paralyzed with fear.

I was going to die. Just like my parents.

But before they could shoot, Reggie and Axel fired. Both men slumped over their steering wheels.

That was about all I could take. I collapsed to my knees in the middle of the street, shaking and crying. My nightmare just wouldn't seem to end.

Strong arms cocooned me, and I looked up to find Spence.

"Oh, my god, Spence, I thought they shot you," I said through my sobs.

"You're safe now, sweetie. They're all dead," he said, pulling me to my feet.

I wiped my tears, still shaking, and saw Jack pulling India by the arm.

"You... you were going to have me killed," I screamed at her. "You were my friend."

She lunged right back at me, her eyes filled with a hatred I didn't know she possessed.

Her face was ugly and tight when she spoke. "You know what it's like being friends with you?" she spat.

What?

"I was a good friend to you—"

She shook her head, her black hair flying around as she tried to pull out of Jack's grip. "You're spoiled and clueless. You have no idea how the world works. You couldn't survive five minutes without your family's money! And you treated me like a charity case. But I was paid a lot of money to lead certain people to you.

When I get away from you creeps—" She paused to look at the four guys. "—I'll finally be rich. I don't need you anymore, Phee!"

I couldn't say a word. My best friend really felt that way about me? How could I have been so stupid?

"You sold me out? And you were in cahoots with Sammy?" I asked quietly.

She rolled her eyes. "What do you think, you idiot? Of course I was. And I fucked him, too!"

I lunged at her again and got a solid smack across her nasty face before Reggie managed to restrain me.

"You'll pay for killing my parents," I said slowly and evenly.

A smile spread across her face, and she laughed. She dropped her head back and laughed even harder, so hard that tears ran down her face. "You're a fool, fucking these dirtbag *mountain men*. You disgust me," she spat.

"All right, enough of that," Reggie said, shaking his head with an amused smile. "Let's get her in the car."

But when we started walking down the driveway, he loosened his grip on my arm. I seized the opportunity to charge at India. With a fist squeezed as tightly as possible, I punched the shit out of her jaw.

I wasn't sure who screamed more loudly—she or I. Excruciating pain shot through my hand as I shook my arm to try and make it go away. Who the hell knew it would hurt so badly to throw a punch? That's not how it worked in the movies.

India got the worst of it, however. Blood trickled

out of the corner of her mouth, and while she wasn't knocked out, her head hung limply from the impact of my fist.

My badass fist.

"I might be a fool," I spat at my former best friend, "but I can fucking *fight*."

CHAPTER 22

SPENCE

"**W**here are they taking her, Spence?" Phee asked, cradling the fist she'd punched India with.

"Don't worry about it. We just need to get out of here," I said. "Reggie, you and Jack take our wannabe assassin lady here, and Axel and I will meet you back at the hotel. Phee, come with me."

She hustled to catch up and jumped in the passenger seat.

"Bet your hand hurts, huh?" I asked.

Trying to straighten her stiff fingers, she said, "Yeah. I need ice."

She twisted to look out the back window where Reggie and Jack were dealing with India.

"They're taking her to a safe place with some of our local operatives. They'll interrogate her and get to the bottom of who's behind all this."

"Will she be okay?" she asked.

This woman blew me away. She was betrayed by a friend in the worst possible way and was still concerned about her. I looked in the rearview mirror and watched my buddies get smaller.

"I don't know, Phee."

"Thank you, Spence."

I stole a look at her, all blotchy and red from crying, but her big eyes and full lips gave her an almost ethereal beauty. Damn, if she didn't leave me with a twitch in my pants.

"Just doing our jobs," I said.

She shook her head. "No, you guys have done way more than your jobs. You've been really, really good to me. I'll make sure Morrow compensates you well."

"*What?*"

"Aren't you guys getting paid—"

Was she kidding?

"You think this is about being paid?" I asked, shocked.

Her mouth opened and closed. "Um, yeah."

"We are not being paid. This is part of what we do—look out for each other's loved ones. We're doing it out of respect for your father's legacy. We'd do anything for him."

"I… I had no idea."

"The minute Morrow called us with the news and

asked if you could stay with us, we began making preparations."

Her hand flew up to her face. "I'm sorry. I didn't know."

There was a lot our girl didn't know.

I couldn't speak for the other guys, but it wasn't until we were all five back up on the mountain that I could really breathe again. We'd been on tougher missions before, but I'm not sure we'd ever faced anything as high stakes as defending the daughter of the man who we all looked up to. And who we were now pretty damn attached to.

Seriously.

We weren't entirely sure the threat against her was eliminated, nor if it would ever be. She might have to go through life looking over her shoulder, being careful when and where she went, always in the company of a security team. That would have to be her new reality.

Ironic that her father, one of the top security guys in the world, created a legacy in need of the very type of services he got so wealthy providing. Because of his work, his daughter would never be entirely safe. At least, not without round-the-clock precautions.

He probably knew that, though, which was why he had Morrow. And us.

So, now we were up at bat, the guys and me.

And it was time to have a serious conversation with our girl.

Back home, we sat around the living room, a couple of us drinking scotch and the rest drinking a nice red wine, when I decided to speak for the group.

"So, Phee, we have something to talk to you about," I said.

Her eyebrows rose. "Really, Spence? What? Am I in trouble? Did I screw something up?"

We laughed. "No, no, nothing like that."

She breathed a sigh of relief. "Okay. Whew."

I jiggled the ice cubes in my scotch to stall. But I knew I just had to get it over with.

"Phee." Cripes, all eyes were on me. "We know you have plans for your life. You want to travel, study art, work on a book, maybe teach."

She nodded.

"We want you to do all that. And we also would like to invite you to stay with us."

Confusion crossed her face. "What do you mean, *us?*" she asked.

I looked at the other guys for support. "We care about you. We all do. A lot. And we'd like you to stay. You know, live with us. Of course, you'll travel and fulfill all your dreams, but we'd like for Savage Mountain to be the place you come home to. Where you'll be with us."

She set her wineglass down, and I braced myself for the worst. The cabin was awesome, as was the mountain, but was it enough for her? Were *we* enough for her?

"I've grown attached to all of you, too, in case you couldn't tell." She blushed deeply. "But if I stayed, I'd feel compelled to choose one of you. And... I don't think I can do that." She looked down at her hands, her voice cracking.

Axel walked over and put an arm around her. "Now, look. This might be a little tricky to get your head around, but from our perspective, you don't actually *have* to choose. We don't want you to choose."

She looked up and sniffled, confusion crossing her face. "I don't know what you mean."

He wove his fingers through hers and brought her hand to his lips for a kiss. "We all want to be with you. You know, share you. We love you, Phee. And we hope you love us, too."

She pulled her hand out of Axel's.

"No. I'd have to choose. And I refuse to do that. I'd rather die alone than hurt one of you."

She turned and started toward her room.

"Wait, Phee," Jack said, jumping to his feet. "At least think about it."

She gave us a sad smile and continued across the courtyard.

Several hours later, I dropped my huge duffel in the

middle of the living room and got a big bear hug from each of the guys.

"Good luck, Spence. We're rooting for you, man," Reggie said.

"Hey, bring us back some good *jamon* or *manchego*," Jack laughed.

I stuffed a couple books in my backpack. "Dude, I'm not going grocery shopping there. I'm going to Spain to pick up my kid."

"What are you guys talking about? Are you going somewhere, Spence?" Phee asked, joining us.

"Hey, baby. I'm glad you're here. I wanted to say goodbye," I said.

Her brow creased. "What do you mean goodbye? Where are you going?"

I laughed. "Spain. And I think by the time I come back, you'll probably be gone."

"What are you going to Spain for?"

I was beaming. Couldn't help it. "I got a call from my private investigator. He found my ex-wife and baby hiding out there."

Her mouth dropped open, and the biggest smile I'd ever seen spread across her face. "No way. Oh, my god, Spence, that's amazing!" She jumped into my arms, screaming.

"You're telling me! I've been walking on clouds since I got the call just a few hours ago."

Seriously. I didn't think I'd been as happy since the day my little girl was born. I was going to be a father again. We'd have a little girl to raise on Savage Mountain.

The guys were all thrilled about being assistant dads. The kid was going to be spoiled rotten.

"When's your flight? Can I go?" she asked.

Huh?

"What do you mean?" I asked.

"Well, I actually wanted to talk to you all you guys for a sec."

"Um. Okay," I said, taking a seat on the sofa, the other guys joining me. And looking equally confused.

She had our attention now.

Phee clasped her hands together. "Guys. I've been thinking, and… I want to accept your invitation."

I looked around the room. If you could have bottled the palpable confusion, it would have overflowed the entire house.

But Phee just smiled at us, that luscious smile, and flipped her blonde hair behind her shoulder. The hair I was dying to grab a fistful of.

But I could wait. A few minutes, anyway.

"Um, Phee, could you repeat that please?" Jack asked.

She laughed. "I'd like to stay here on Savage Mountain, if the invitation still stands. I thought about it and realized how much I care about each of you. I love you… all four of you. I've known it for a while but was trying to deny it. Thank you for not making me choose."

Jack jumped to his feet. "Are you kidding?" he yelled, smiling. "That's great news!"

He picked her up and spun her around.

"Are you sure? I mean really sure this is what you want?" he asked.

My question exactly.

She nodded, wearing a huge grin. "I am sure. I want to be here with all of you. I really do."

We all jumped up and took turns kissing our girl and hugging each other.

What a day. First, I find out I'm getting my little girl back, and then, I find out my grown-up girl wants to stick around.

It couldn't get much better than that. Although, with all of us living under one roof on Savage Mountain, I knew things were going to be pretty goddamn special.

EPILOGUE

Phee emerged from the water, long hanks of blonde hair clinging to her like a second skin. She was holding the hand of Spence's little girl, Abby, whose blonde hair clung to her like she was Phee's mini-me.

Amazing.

We'd decided to all go to Spain together to celebrate finding Abby, and to welcome Phee into our lives. And now that our two special ladies had met, they were inseparable.

Spence had been worried about Abby's adjustment to

living without her mother. But he explained to the little tyke that Momma was going away for a while, and that now it was his turn to be her parent. There were tears and a couple sleepless nights, but thanks to lots of love and attention, the kid was adjusting to her new family.

We'd been staying in a lovely villa in San Sebastian for a month, swimming in the ocean by day and eating delicious pinxtos and other Basque treats by night. Morrow had even joined us for a week for a partial vacation-work trip. He wanted to discuss security arrangements, naturally.

Honestly, Phee couldn't be in better hands. I mean, four special ops dudes, experts in private security? Being with us was like having your own private Secret Service. Morrow had just wanted to button down some of the details of how things would work. It was everyone's priority to keep Phee safe, yet not make her feel like a prisoner. She had a life to live, and we planned to live it with her.

But our time in San Sebastian was coming to a close. We gradually realized how much we missed Savage Mountain and how it was our real home.

Sure, we'd come and go, experiencing other parts of the world, but we'd always come back to the mountain to recharge and remind ourselves how lucky we were.

And now that we had little Abby to look after, it was more important than ever that we made sure the cabin was a real home. But with Phee's touch, we were confident we'd make it work.

We still had a lot to learn, but we were a family, and nothing would ever change that.

DID YOU LIKE *The Pursued*?
Learn about the next book in the collection,
THE PRIZE

I hope you loved reading this book as much as I
loved writing it.
Find all Mika Lane books here:
https://mikalaneshop.com/

Dear Reader:

I'm USA TODAY bestselling romance author Mika Lane, and am OBSESSED with bringing you sassy, steamy stories with imperfect heroines and the bad-a*s dudes they bring to their knees. I'll always bring you my signature humor and heat, topped off with a modern-day happily ever after.

My first book ever was *The Day I Ate the Milkyway*, a true fourth-grade masterpiece illustrated with crayons and bound with construction paper and glue. Nowadays, steamy romance gives purpose to my days and nights as I create worlds and characters that tickle the imagination. I live in magical Northern California with my own handsome alpha dude, sometimes known as Mr. Mika Lane, and two devilish cats named Chuck and Murray.

A dual citizen of the United States and Ireland, I have on more than one occasion spent my last dollar on a plane ticket somewhere, and am always planning my next escape. I often try new recipes on unsuspecting friends, search out hiding places to read undisturbed, and sadly kill every houseplant I bring home.

I LOVE to hear from readers when I'm not dreaming up naughty tales to share. Visit my online shop https://mikalaneshop.com/ and say hello https://mikalaneshop.com/pages/meet-mika.

xoxo, Mika